With Time Shall Freedom Bring...

By

James M. Keel

ISBN: 1-4107-9084-3 (e-book)
ISBN: 1-4107-9085-1 (Paperback)

This book is printed on acid free paper.

1stBooks - rev. 08/30/03

Preface

This is the story of the immortality of eight men, which through out history develop the freemen of the world, and along this timeless journey become the founders of a democratic society...or two.

Chapter One

It was early in the morning as Adsideo watched the Chinese man hose down his area of the sidewalk in front of the opera house and yelled at the pedestrians as he did every morning.

This had become a ritual to Adsideo to rise early and watch and listen to the comments from the passers by to the little old man.

The Chinese man had owned the news, slash shoeshine stand for over forty years. Adsideo spoke with him each day for a few moments while he picked up his copy of the local newspaper.

The old man had apparently been around for a long time and so had Adsideo. Though it was not apparent to just anyone. He and the others like him knew the truth.

Adsideo was tall, dark headed, and stout. He had been born in the ancient city of Tyre in 1063 B.C. And the average person would have said upon meeting Adsideo that he was in his mid to late forty's. He had the look of a Spanish nobleman and the wealth twice that of any of the remaining royalty left on earth at this time.

He was in very good health for his 2900 some odd years old. This had proven to be a curse as well as a blessing.

But this morning was different for tonight they were to meet for dinner and discuss the progress made since the "event." This brought back passed memories of other places and other times.

Maybe it was the weather and the way Geary Street looked that morning.

As he looked over Union Square. It reminded him of the view of the "vicus Iugarius" and the path leading up to and around the Basilca Iulia of the once young city of Rome.

Many a time as a senator, he had walked though the forum and would pass this way to the senate. Passed the column of Phocas and the other honorary columns marking a victory of one or another he had walked.

Passed the Lacus Curtius, then the golden Milestone, and on towards Castor & Pollux.

It would be there at the intersection of Vicus Tuscus and the Via Sacra, that he would watch the children sell pigeons for the days up coming bird fights.

There would be the windows above, which were always open at the house of the vestal virgins. This would always be good for a rise early in the morning, as they would speak out to all the passers by. They would giggle and taunt each other and pretend to look noticeable.

Sometimes they were down at the street level giving their maidens a case of high blood pressure as they would try and speak with the passersby face to face as the Nutes pulled them back inside.

He would then cross over to the temple of Antoninius & Faustina and pretend to pray for their well being and give offerings to the priests.

But he knew that these Gods of theirs was only someone's insecurities and or some way to rationalize how and why we as men existed.

He served the one God whose face he had seen and voice he had heard so long ago.

The God of the Abraham. For you see Adsideo had served one of his true sons before the" Event". The son of David, the golden and gifted son of David. Solomon had been his name. That's right he had served as the captain of the royal guard. He and the other seven like him had all served as the royal guard, the others were under Adsideo, but never the less they were all of the same brotherhood.

These had been memories that were cherished as he now watched his new modern nation that he and the others had so carefully helped to found, of then and now. Rome and this United States of America had become the two greatest on earth and he hoped that this one would not fall to the strong and ignorant as the past one had.

The outlook was the same it seemed. For as in the past as in the present the problems of drugs, racism, corruption, and just plain laziness were abound.

The people just become to trusting and content.

As he had said under a different name at a different time to a different crowd "there should be a tax revolt every 10 to 15 years to keep your politicians honest and the government in check".

There were eight others like him on the planet at this time, as there had been since that first time of the "event" as he had learned to call it. One of those was God almighty himself. The other seven are always close at hand and forever watching as Adsideo did himself.

Adsideo had been born into a family of soldiers and training began very early in those days. At seven years of age his uncle had sent him to the priest for training as a warrior cleric.

He had at first been sent to the home of the then young King's guards and taught to protect the temple with his honor and his life if it came to that.

As he learned his trade he also learned that it would often come to that calling of the guard and he would see numerous of his fellow trainee's fall to the blade during training alone.

As the King grew older so did Adsideo. Soon after his 17th year he would see the King begin a triumphant feat of building as directed by God himself.

It was a golden time, literally. He was now in charge of the guarding of the master builder and the King himself. Sometimes when the beautiful queen from the far away land of Sheba would come to see the King, he was allowed into the great temple room itself. To guard there conversations from prying ears and eyes.

He loved this room with the great cherubs that stood wing tip to wing tip and floor to ceiling ushering in the holy will of God himself. The walls and grand columns and everything were covered in bronze and gold. There were engravings of cherubs, palm trees, and open flowers on all of the walls. All of which were overlaid with gold. There were massive doors leading into the tabernacle, which was engraved with the cherubs, palm trees and open flowers as well. And this was also overlaid with gold.

Now that the time had passed and he was able to remember this grand time he knew now that it had really been God himself that spoke with the King.

Once while at his post he had heard a conversation in the tabernacle and was caught by the high priest on his way in to the vestibule. Later the next day this was brought before the King's attention.

The King asked if he had heard what was said and he replied with the truth, that he could not make out what was said. The King knowing this to be true invited him into the room of the tabernacle and allowed him to see the rooms contents and he spoke into the room before they entered to tell God that he was being allowed to do so, since he was now to become the captain of the internal guard to keep all away from it's treasures. He could not believe he was allowed into this room without it causing his death. This had always been the warning given to him by the previous captain of the guard whom had trained him.

That should anyone pass though the doorway to this room would surely die from the wraith of God. This had been seen in the generations passed by the eyes of our fathers. The high priest, Aaron's sons had been burned to death by the wraith of God.

Their only discretion was that they entered the tent of meeting ahead of their father and it had cost them their lives. Now there were trials that would require walking past the doorway while God sat within. It was said that if you were to turn your head into the light that you would be turned into ash.

Inside the room were the tabernacle and the throne with the horns that were anointed with the blood of that days sacrifice. Next to this was a table and a candleholder and assorted furnishings.

Behind this area was another area that had been divided by a huge curtain.

The King told him that he would never be allowed behind this curtain. He told him that only when God himself was in the house could the King view what was known as the "Ark of the covenant".

The King then told him that this was a gift given to the Lord by Moses and that it contained the tablets with the laws of our people. These had been written by the hand of God himself and would strike down the enemy of our people should the Ark be taken into battle.

He remembered now that he had been so frightened that he asked to be excused in fear that the Lord would come into the room and strike him down. He was to learn of this objects power later in his life.

Now the King had a great passion for women of all shapes and colors. There would be hundreds a month that would visit his palace across the plaza from where his post was. He would see so many that he could not imagine the stamina of the King. From this he fathered many children and many of these were sons. Surely he would be the most powerful King of the land. This would later be his discretion to God. And lead to his loss of his health.

He served this King until the King's death when they were both long into their lives. He knew that he would surely be laid with his fathers soon after the King was laid to rest.

Now during the reign of the beloved King their Kingdom was the wealthiest ever known to man and the most powerful army was at his disposal. For all of the soldiers loved there fair and just King and would have given their lives at his command. But after the death of their beloved King, his son that was to follow his reign, was spoiled in the wealth and was not in the favor of our Lord.

Adsideo on the other hand had been blessed by his King before his death and was given the post of the captain of the royal guard.

He branded his legions as the royal temple guard and trained them very hard day in and day out. They had been made up of the artisans and masons that had built the house of God and the royal palace. And from this they were strong at heart and great in will.

They were to become the strongest and most dedicated of all legions.

The outer posts of the Kingdom soon notified the new King that an invasion by the Egyptian King Shishak was underway and that he would need to dispatch the army as soon as they could be made ready for battle. Adsideo had asked that he be sent to manage the battle plan but was told that he was to stay and defend the holy city. The King himself would ride to the field and over see the battle first hand. He begged that his orders be changed but without prevail.

Now as he stood watch over the palace compound with his buckle and sword as his armament waiting and watching for the messengers from the front line. Adsideo was tall and proud to have been on the wall at such a time even though he would have been in the King's place.

The King and the main body of the troops had been gone for days now and yet no word had arrived as to their success.

Adsideo' s men were on the wall and through out the compound. He had a hard time lately keeping their moral up. They too were ready for battle and would rather have been the first at the battlefield defending their King. He had inspired them by marching them into the King's palace and showing some of them for the first time the gold overlay and the throne room it's self.

They were aggressive after this and he lead them to the cook's quarters for a huge meal to keep their minds from the battle, but to also remind them of their mighty King's wealth.

Now as he stood on the wall all he could think about was battle. Adsideo was a great general at this point. He was graying in his beard but still dark in hair, tall and wide in the chest. He wore his usual breastplate with the cherub design like the huge statues in the house of God. Sandals and shin plates were worn, as did all of the men.

He did not wear the helmet that was issued to the other soldiers, he did not like this, and it cut off his perifial view and was hot and somewhat heavy on top of that.

He favored the blue and gold headdress of his family's robes and wore this as a marker for his men so that in battle he was easily identified.

He hated waiting! If only the messenger he had dispatched to the frontline would return or maybe even a triumphant King. But this was not to be the case today or forever more. The King would not return today nor would Adsideo ever see his dead master's son again.

Right as the evening sun came down on the horizon he saw a dust cloud that was formed by thousands of troops traveling at what appeared to be great speed. It also appeared that they would reach the temple-fortress at dusk. Adsideo did not have to sound the alert since several of his men saw the same thing at about the same time. The men began calling in all of the troops, children, and fathers that had been grazing the cattle and preparing for the next days sacrifices.

All of the youngest of the children and women had been sent up to Nabulus before the King had rode off in his journey to meet the pharaoh. The gates were bolted, portals shut and barricaded, and the lamps were lit. The messengers were sent to retrieve the men that were farther out to our south. He sent orders for these troops to swing around to the Jordan, follow it southward, turn west, and through the mountain pass at Mt. Scopus. From here they were to hit the Egyptians from the valley of Kidron and cause them to split both southwesterly and back through the valley of Hinnom, where his strongest of the Royal Guard would have a trap set for them. As the sun grew closer to the horizon, Adsideo and his mounted troops road through the stables and out the southern gate toward Mt. Ophel and due west. There they turned past Mt. Zion and stood at King David's tomb where they would await the pharaoh's troops.

Chapter Two

Near midnight a message was received as expected that revealed that the Egyptians had reached the temple compounds outer wall. Now they would have to wait for his troops from the northern sectors to advance through the valley of Hinnom and push them through the valley and toward the tomb of David. The night was restless and the winds blew through the valley and into their faces. This was causing a whistle of the rock face and it sounded distraught. They listened to it, as they were as silent as they could be. The horses were quite restless and caused even more stress on the men. As the night lingered into morning he sent a dispatch toward the temple compound. As he waited the return of this messenger he began to doubt himself for leaving the palace. What if they were to over throw his main body of troops and be received into the house of God? No this could not happen. This had been his context of thought when so quickly devising this plan, God would take care of his own he had thought.

As the time grew near for the return of his messengers Adsideo sensed something wrong and ordered his men back through the valley and towards the palace walls. He ordered them at full speed. To ride on ahead of each other as fast as possible, and that battle would be expected.

As they reached the perimeter walls at daybreak the Egyptian camp was not to be seen, but in its place his troops from the northern sector slaughtered. The southern gates were gone as well. The invaders were in the palace compound. He ordered his men to ride to the gate. He would block their exit and then reclaim the palace ground. As they approached the gates, they could see that the

Egyptians had massacred the entire interior Guard as well. No one was left alive!

No one could be seen moving about!

Into the palace grounds they rode when suddenly one of the gates fell over onto its side and blocked the gate opening cutting off all of his men from entering except for two to threescore that had been right behind him. Then he could hear the order of retreat by his men that were outside of the palace walls, for it seemed that the Egyptians had set up an ambush and were in pursuit of his men. His horse reared up and made a circle as he pulled back on the reins and began ordering his men to throw their ropes onto the gate and ride in support of their fellow soldiers. They pulled the gate down rather quickly only to see that the remaining troops that had been on the other side were being slaughtered.

Most of the remaining men that had been trapped in the palace walls with him were now riding into the battle. He could not get their attention to retreat back into the palace in time before the Egyptians flanks began to turn back out to their respective sides and return to the rear and envelope the remaining guard and butchered them as well.

Now with only a handful of men left they scurried to the palace, for now the Egyptians were starting towards the palace gate and into the palace compound once again. Adsideo and his men reached the temple and began to bar the doors. It would only be a few minutes before the pharaoh's men would reach the doors.

He thought of the Ark! He began to order the men that were still with him to follow as they headed for the tabernacle. The dwelling place of God.

The golden doors were open! Adsideo lead the way in and as soon as the last man was over the threshold the doors slammed shut and the lamps were blown out!

As they stopped in the dark to try and get their bearings a voice spoke out to them.

"Hear me Templar Guards! As I have told your forefathers shall I tell you!

I the God of your father Abraham, as the God of your King David, and the God of your King Solomon. Hear this now and do as I command of you!

Your King, Rehoboam I have caused to fall today, as my chosen ones have also fallen.

They have not walked in my ways as in my covenant with Israel. And has caused them to sin!

Now they will be lead back into Egypt as bondmen where I had freed them from once before! Into bondage they will be lead! For you few, you shall take the Ark unto Sinai where the tablets were received by your father Moses. They shall not once more fall into the hands of the non-believers!

Carry the Ark as directed by me to your fathers before you. Sing the praise of my name as you go before and behind, and never look back for you shall fear anything! I shall be with you and will be seen following you as a powerful cloud of dust by day and a wind of fire by night. Fear not for I will protect you!

There will I grant you my will, and you will be rewarded greatly!

Slowly the doors began to open again and light flooding the room showing each man the startled face of the other. The men stood there for a moment trying to understand what had happened. An eerie silence hung in the air. Adsideo looked up at the other men looking at him, he knew at that moment that what they had been chosen for was far more greater then anything that could be imagined. Snapping back to reality, and knowing that time was lacking Adsideo and the others grabbed the wooden poles and slid them into the Ark and picked it up. They then carried it out of the room of meeting into the temple. As they approached the temple door they could hear the Egyptians pulling at the door with ropes. At that moment a bolt of fire shot from the Ark and burned a hole through the doors sending the Egyptians falling backwards!

They rushed into the plaza and ran for the gates when the cloud of God swept in behind them and disintegrated the Egyptian soldiers. They ran through the gates and exited the temple compound into the city. They then headed for the southern gates and exited through the magnificent Water gates. Little did Adsideo know at the time but it would be several hundred years before he would return to the beloved city of David. And when he did he would never see it like it had been before this day. As they headed into the valley of the son of Hinnom Adsideo noticed that the entire battlefield was cleared and all that remained was the weaponry and empty chariots that were scattered everywhere. There was not a single scrap of clothing or a body of man or horse.

They continued to march the Ark through the valley and into the night. They would stop briefly to change out carrying the Ark. Never did they look behind them heeding to the word of God. As dusk turned to night they could see the fiery presents of God by the light that was cast ahead of them as they traveled.

The next morning they were told by God to hide in a near by cave and to do so by daylight and to travel by night.

Chapter Three
(The others)

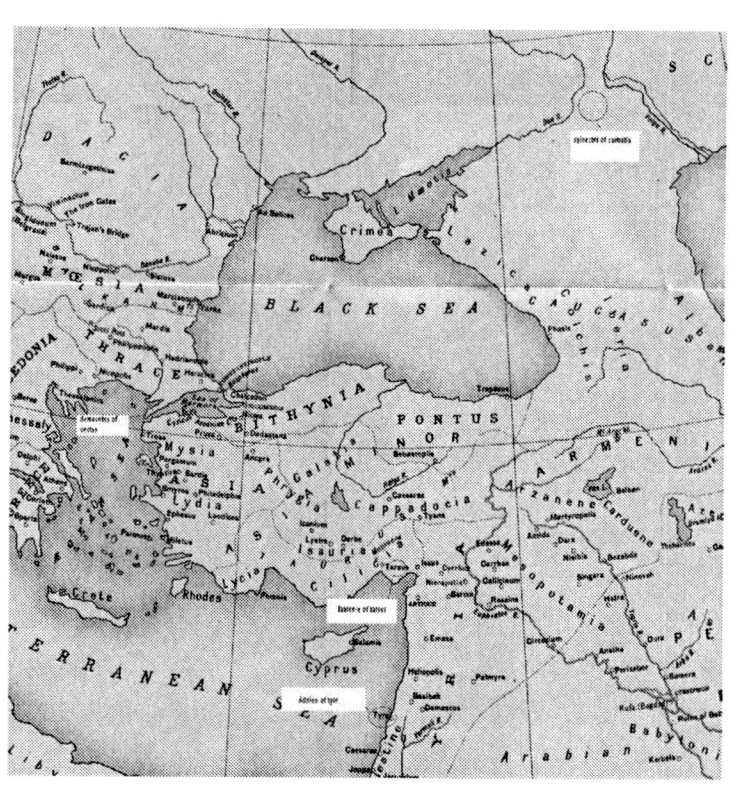

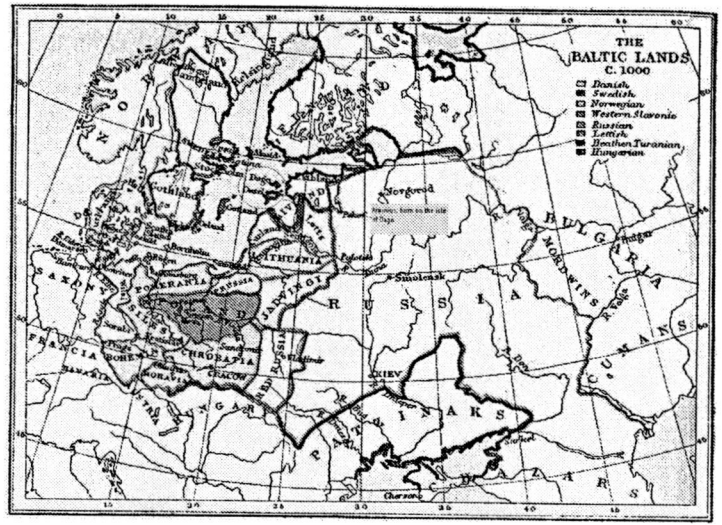

After Adsideo and the others woke near sunset they began to realize the reasons God himself had selected each of them. Each had special skills in protection or physical knowledge.

There was Sylvester, Maurice, Laurence, Democritus, Arminus, Colin, and Dominic.

Sylvester, the big burly bearded woodsman type with long blonde hair, stood towering over most men. He was in his early forties with a red sun beaten face due to his fair skin with a light hazel eye color. He was good at building and had joined the guard after being imported to the palace during the construction. He had loved the temple so much that he would not leave so that is why he decided to join, so he would be able to guard it the rest of his life. He was originally brought, not for his strength, which he had plenty of, but because of his skills as a mason and carpenter. He had been one of the most important to King Solomon before his death. He was born in the region that is

15

nearest to the Vyatka and Kama River's called Cheremis, presently tucked in between the Don and the Volga Rivers.

Maurice was the scout for the guards and was a keen hunter of man and animal. He was as strong winded as any a man you would ever meet and could run very long distances.

He was a large man with ebony skin and dark black hair that hung just above his shoulders. His face lacking of any hair, was strong, with dark blue eyes. He was of the peoples that would later in history be known as the Moors. During times of peace and construction of the temple and palace he had supplied the meals for the craftsman. He had come into the service of King Solomon during a campaign in to Pelusuim. It was there that the Kings of the two regions decided that there would be games of the champions to decide who was the better in military skills.

Now Maurice was the best archer of his King's troops and had never been beaten in the previous games. Little did he know but the King had long since been the trainer of his Royal guard's archers and was regarded as his Kingdoms best archer.

It was the end of the games and the final challenge was the archery. Now Maurice was up ahead of the Hebrew archer and shot a perfect arrow into the center of the human effigy's skull.

The King rose up and asked to be given his bow and arrow. He took aim and shot his arrow right above but exactly in the same place as Maurice's arrow had been placed. You could not have slid a heads hair in between the two arrows.

The King of Pelusuim contested since Solomon had not been expected to enter the games and everyone knew that he had been anointed by his God as King, why having this blessing was to treat the Pelusuim' S as fools.

Finally after quite an argument Solomon agreed to secede in this contest and Maurice and Pelusuimities was ruled the victors.

Now Solomon and his men were to leave immediately and did so without habituating.

As they were leaving the city Maurice asked if he could ride with the army on it's journey back to the southwest lands. He was given permission by Solomon to remain with the King for as long as Maurice was to ride with the King and keep him company for Solomon believed that Maurice was a spy or an assassin and wanted to keep a close eye on this foreigner. He also had asked Adsideo to watch him as well.

Soon after, Maurice earned the trust of the King and became a trusted companion to the King.

Laurence was a noted advisor and negotiator for the King and served in the throne room during civil and foreign matters. He had been an ambassador to Tarsus appointed by Solomon since this had been Laurence's place of birth. Laurence was also a noted poet and philosopher with dark curly hair and fair skin and light brown eyes. He was short in height but big in knowledge. Now in his upper forties, he had been a student of Levian a philosopher at the school of political science at Tarsus, sent there as a very young boy, and was a passionate writer of his times. He charted every journey he took and wrote a journal every day.

Democritus was a Thracian from the great city of Sestus and had also been schooled at a higher society school. He had been taught under the great Homer of Smyrna. Though he was not inspired to become a writer of tales he was known to tell a few. He had been inspired to become an adventurer and had searched out every avenue to go to the farthest reaches of the civilized world and then some.

Now at the youthful age of thirty-five years of age he was one of the two youngest in the group and full of ideas. He was rather tall for a Thracian and had the golden skin like the Latians, and dark eyes. He had curly blond hair that was kept neatly cut. Under King Solomon he was the explorer of foreign lands and an artisan of maps. Eventually he was regarded as the King's ambassador to all external affairs.

He had also written annuals of the great feats of material acquisitions and deliveries that had been accomplished by Sylvester during the construction of the temple and Palace.

Arminius was a man in his late forties, strong and battle tough. He was born in the northland on the isle of Dago. He was born to a warrior family of great maritime skills as well as hand-to-hand combat training. His specialty was maritime navigational skills and ship building techniques. He was studied as any in the mapping of the stars and in their seasonal movements. He had been on a pillaging quest for treasures when he and his crew had lost to a battle with the sea. This had been off of the coasts of Carpathia and Rhodes. He and one of his crew had survived the disaster. Once on shore at Rhodes they found out quickly that they were not welcomed by any means. They were captured and in prisoned in the port city's dungeon. Now Arminius was a large red headed man with a baby face that set off his light blue eyes. But he did not fear anything known to him. He was confident from the beginning that he would easily gain his freedom. This was not to be the case. He was eventually sold into bondage to a Lycian shipbuilder and found himself working in the shipyards at Phoenix.

It was through this that he was soon sold to bondsman to Sylvester during the building of the temple. This had happened once Sylvester had learned of his navigational skills he gave Arminius his freedom as a bargain that he would serve in the completion of the temple by overseeing all of the imported materials by sea. After the completion of the temple Arminius had remained at the service of the King and the Royal Guard as the Naval advisor.

Colin was the second of the younger members. He was a Pict from the Isle of Skye.

He was of the Pickens clan and was of noble stock. He was fair in height with mid length blonde hair and bright green eye's. His family was the original landholders of the Isle and had other land holdings on the mainland. Colin had twelve brothers and one sister. Her name had been Lucia. Colin being the youngest of all had never met his mother. She had died during Colin's birth. His father still blamed Colin for this, and had not cared for the boy at all. They hardly spoke. Even now Colin could not remember his father ever having touched him.

At age twelve his sister had taken Colin to their grandfather and asked him what to do with the boy. She was only eight years older than Colin but appeared much older.

Since their mother had passed she had ran their estate's house beginning at the age of twelve. Her father had given up on the family holdings and drank most of the time.

Lucia took young Colin to their Grandfather. She needed to be assured of the boy's safety.

Their grandfather's name was Drake Of Pickens, he was in his seventy-fifth year, and he was the family monarch.

Lucia cried to her grandfather as they spoke of Colin that night at Drake's Craig, as the house was known in those days.

"The older brothers would not have anything to do with the young boy and they cursed him and threw stones and food at Colin" she had cried to her grandfather. They too blamed Colin for the death of their mother but even more for the fall of their father's, by his own fault never less, and loss of respect with the other nobles.

Now as Lucia had cried to her grandfather for someone who would take the boy. Lucia wanted to leave her fathers estate and could not take the boy with her. She was going to marry and needed to "rid herself of him" she said.

Now this infuriated Drake "he is a Pickens, not a dog" he said, "this is my grandson and I will care for him. I will go down to your fathers house and speak with him tomorrow".

Drake told his granddaughter to leave that night for if he sees her in his sight come morning he would send her back to her father in a coffin. He was fed up with the sight of her he had said.

Drake went into the hall and pulled Colin up from the bench outside the door and carried him to the guest quarters and sat him down.

He had told Colin that night that there would never be any harm done to him ever again.

Even today as he thought of that night he felt loved again by the words of his grandfather, but it would not be much longer in his life when he was on his own once again. Now tonight with the other men of the guard he knew this was his family. They depended on him as much as he depended on them and he like the brotherhood. Colin had come to the royal guard as a guest.

He had traveled to the temple with the queen of Sheba during her second visit to Solomon. He was an interpreter for the queen to the Greek nations of the east and north of her country.

Once Colin had visited the temple site he asked to stay after the queen left, with her permission of course, to study in the Kings library. He had heard of the tale of their exodus out of bondsman ship in Egypt and was fascinated by this and the feeling he had from this palace.

He felt enlightened somehow and had an incorrigible desire for the knowledge of this palace and it's many manuscripts from foreign nations. These were gifts from the many bearers of homage from their respective countries and what an assortment of gifts they were.

Colin from that time on served as an advisor to the King, and Laurence as needed.

Dominic of Caer-Fyrddin was the last of the eight that would soon witness the "event".

Dominic was of royal stock. He had been the lone son of an Anglo nobleman. Unlike the younger guards that stood with him tonight Dominic was not the younger of the guards. He was in his sixty-sixth year and was still able to ride a full day, just not as easily as before. He was tall in height with a slender build. His hair, long and graying, was worn back in a loose ponytail. He was unable to bear the Ark so he carried the wineskins for the others.

Now Dominic had been a student of magic and natural arts before hearing of the God of Abraham. He had traveled for three years to reach the temple from his homeland. Once he had learned all he could from the Levites, he was converted from his druid background into the way of the Lord By walking in the way of the light.

This had been the ceremony of walking in the presents of the Lord in an act of faith without fear.

He would never forget that night. The doors had been open to the tabernacle; the glow from inside the room into the hall from Dominic's view was immense. He could here the voice as it spoke to one of the son's of Benjamin. He walked slowly towards the door and into the doorway being careful not to turn and look into the light. As he passed into the light he could feel love, pure love and assurance. Light so bright he could feel it throughout his body and he liked it. It was joy and enlightenment.

He knew after that, that he could use the powers of natural science as long as he did not provoke the power of God by the worship of a false or evil entity. For he now knew that there was only one God and he had been the only one ever.

These powers were revealed to him even more so than before due to his understanding of the universe. He became more knowledgeable and more powerful in his faith to God with the science of the Ark. It was taught to only the select of guards and took much patience to walk before the Ark. Undoubting faith to march into the face of your enemy and watch as God destroyed all unfaithful in the path of the Ark. The words of the psalm that were spoken were sacred and taught by the Levite priest by generation. Dominic was devoted to the protection of the Ark and knew that his survival was not fate.

Chapter Four

Now as dusk settled into the night Adsideo and the others brought the Ark out and covered it with grass and twigs to disguise it. They began their journey to Ashdod by the sea the first two nights after they left the valley of Himmon. By the third night they were to Ashkelon, now it was here that they heard from the talk in the street, that Shishok had removed all of the remaining items from the tabernacle and everyone assumed that the Ark was also on its way to Egypt as well.

From there they traveled down the coastline to Raphia the following night. Then on to Rhinocolura the night after that. Finally they reached the home of Maurice, Pelusuim by the sea.

There they used the wilderness of Shur to further hide their movements.

Maurice had many friends in Pelusuim and told Adsideo that he, Arminius, and Democritus would go and try to get horses and food for the remainder of the journey.

Into the city they went and what a busy city it was. Sitting in the Nile delta it was a port city that also had a large farmers and livestock market. Now to Arminus it was a great reminder of his past voyages at sea and all of the port cities he had been too as a Norseman. He used to visit his victim cities in disguise before attacking and plundering them at night.

Maurice led them to the old friends house at the end of the cities northern gates. There they met with Axius a livery merchant, and a very old and dear friend from long ago." Maurice my old friend where have you been?" It has been a long time since I saw you last. I thought you had left for good, following the Hebrew King with only one God." Axius laughed before he continued, "We all thought you were smarter than that. Come into the house and I will have a place for you to rest. You look tired," He told them as he led them to his home.

Once inside Axius's home they sat and were greeted with food and wine.

Axius said to Maurice after they had sat down at the table, which was in the middle of the room they stood in. "how have you been old friend"

Maurice replied, "I have never been better in heart and soul but I am in need of your help"

"How can I help you, I would do anything for my old friend, as long as it does not mean the end of my business here or emptying my coffers" replied Axius.

"The King of Egypt has stolen away with the Hebrew treasures and we are headed there to reclaim them. We need your best horses and a couple of burden animals," said Maurice.

This disturbed Axius since Shishok, King of Egypt, was one of his best clients. Axius supplied many of his horses to this Kingdoms army.

"I do not know about this said Axius, if the King should find out I would be put out of business and possibly exiled by the governor".

"You worry too much old friend," said Maurice. I would never betray you or your family like that," said Maurice.

"This will be our secret to my death said Maurice. Now please I need your help".

Axius thought for a moment and then said, "Your death may not be faraway if you intend on facing Shishok!" "Now I do not have enough horses to supply an army but I could have a few hundred in a couple of weeks if you can wait"

"We only need eight horses and a couple of mules. We do not have any time to spare, we must ride out tonight at dusk" said Maurice.

"Only eight well I have that many at the stables, only the best for you my friend" spouted out Axius "you shall have them in no time".

"There is only one price I will accept from you my friend". Said Axius.

"What would that be?" asked Maurice "that you come back to your old friends and you're place of birth to sail terra cotta ships with me" replied Axius.

"All right! It is a deal," said Maurice.

He had not thought of this for sometime. When they were both boys they would play with the ships and dream of becoming great sailors of the sea.

Why they had sailed these ships behind this very house.

Maurice's mother would make these ships in her Killen. She had been a potter for the town back in those days. She would make the small boats for Maurice on his birthday and would always make one for his friend Axius. They were the only two in the whole town that would get these elegantly detailed ships. Even though she had had some nice offers, from the other parents, to make these for the other children, she never would make them for anyone else until the first time that Maurice did not show any interest in the boats any longer. That was on his thirteenth birthday he remembered. After that his mother began to make and sell a few more of these tiny ships and all of a sudden some of the sailors had bought them, then the other merchant ships were asking for them as well. It seemed that the news of these ships had made its way to Greece and every little boy from Mediterranean Sea to Persia wanted one.

At that time Maurice and his sister had to go into the family business and help it keep up. They even had to buy added help to keep up with the orders for these ships alone and soon they were stopping the production of the dishes and pots. Once that happened it was ships alone that were being dried in the Killen. Even to this day Maurice's sister ran this pottery shop and was still selling the ships. But in these days she had to begin to sell pots and dishes also. Now Maurice knew that it would not be until his return to Pelsium that he would be able to speak with his sister. One, because he did not want to endanger her and second, because there was not anytime for this.

He knew that he must hurry back to Shur and meet back up with Adsideo and the others.

Back at the camp Dominic was speaking to the others. He was asking about their route to the mountain.

"Don't worry" little brother said Sylvester. "we will make it soon enough and safely if I have my way about it" "Aye, aye I shall second that, without any disagreement from any of you, I would place a wager on that" said Laurence.

Adsideo was listening but was also watching for Maurice and the others. They should be back soon. It was only a few hours before dark and they would need to pack the Ark onto the animals. That is if Maurice was successful in obtaining them.

"What will be our route"? Asked Sylvester.

"We will travel down the caravan road," replied Adsideo.

Sylvester was wondering to himself why they were traveling down the very border of the Kingdom that was on the hunt for them. He was about to ask when Dominic beat him to it.

"Because disguised as merchants leaving a market city and traveling so close to Egypt no one will even pays us the slightest bit of attention" Replied Adsideo "we will go to Arsinoe and then turn into the mountain at the pass of Mitla and then though the mountain passes. We will vanish, no one will find us once we make it out of Arsinoe"

Chapter Five

Maurice, Axius, Democritus, and Arminius reached the stables and began to pack two mules and prepared the horses. Axius son Almedus had been sent to get food and water for them to take with them. It did not take him long and once he was back they began to prepare to leave.

Maurice promised that he would return and he asked Axius to let his sister know that he had been in the city and would return as soon as he was finished with his vow.

"Of course Maurice, do not worry everything will be taken care of" promised Axius "you take care of your business and I will take care of your sister"

Democritus and Arminius led the way toward the southern gate followed by Maurice, and then they headed east to Shur. As their train of animals became a spec on the horizon Axius was dispatching a letter to Shishok telling him of the visitors that he had today and the direction in which they had rode in. They did not make it to the camp until almost midnight. Adsideo was waiting, he seemed angry when he spoke to them as they rode up to the camp. Laurence, Sylvester, Colin, and Dominic were all asleep.

"What took to long, did you meet up with someone who did not want to let you go" he said.

"Nothing out of the usual" said Maurice; "we did get all of the animals and some food and water for the journey".

"Well it is just as well, but now we will have to travel during the day until we reach the mountain". Said Adsideo.

"No we will have a short journey for the rest of tonight. Then we will rest during the day. Just as God said to us in the Temple" Maurice quickly replied. "We cannot depend on the safety of disguise alone. We should obey God's advice"

"You are right" Adsideo said to Maurice.

Arminius and Democritus tied the horses and mules up and fed and watered them for they knew that the fresher the horses the better they would be.

Maurice told Adsideo of his old friend and the fact that he had noticed a few of the Egyptian soldiers but not anything out of the ordinary while at Pelsium.

"You three get some rest," said Adsideo "I will wake the others in a couple of hours to help load the Ark and we will be on our way at the next sunset"

"I agree," replied Maurice "I am tired and need rest"

Maurice made sure that the others would have some of the food supplies once they were awakened.

Then Maurice, Arminius, and Democritus lay down by the others and went to sleep.

Now Arminius was the first of the three to fall asleep.

He began to dream of a cave with a very large set of interconnecting chambers.

The ceiling was very high up it seemed, and it twinkled like tiny stars above his head.

He noticed that they were the constellations from the night sky painted on the ceiling. It seemed to be in such detail that he thought he saw glimmers of light from the stars.

Arminius walked through the mouth of the cave and through the tunnels. He kept yelling someone's name but he could not hear himself speak and he seemed confused!

He began to follow the corridors until he came to a large room with a flowing fountain in the middle of the floor. He could see from the entry into the room that this was some kind of a throne room. There was an assortment of golden treasures everywhere he looked!

He began to see behind the throne that there were tapestries hanging over the walls. He also noticed that the engraved wall below these tapestries looked like the palm trees, open flowers, and cherubs of the temple of the tabernacle. "It was the doors to the tabernacle!" He thought to his self.

"Come on Arminius," said as Laurence, as he kicked the feet of the sleeping giant.

"Let's get going."

"Alright, I am getting up! You don't have to kick me!" yelled Arminius.

"Hey calm down" Laurence replied as he climbed onto his horse "you sure are grumpy when you are awakened"

"I am sorry," said Arminius "I was having a dream that was quite peaceful and you surprised me out of my sleep"

Colin spoke out "hey, lets go!"

"It sounds like everyone woke up in a very bad mood," said Dominic.

"I am coming," said Arminius.

As they rode out onto the road to the gulf they rode in single file. Led by Maurice who was followed by Dominic, Adsideo, Laurence, Colin, Democritus, Sylvester, and last of all the sleepy Arminius.

They did not see but two other sets of travelers while on the road that first night.

That day they camped next to a great lake. Dominic took care of refilling the water vessels, Maurice and Arminius hunted for fish & shellfish along the shoreline, and the others erected the tents & took care of the animals.

Democritus saw the Egyptians first and yelled out to the others.

There were three chariots and five horsemen. As they rode up Laurence could see by the markings of the plumage on the horses that these were the pharaoh's elite fighting force, the Nubian royal guards.

The leader of the group, which numbered eleven in all, began to speak.

"What are your names and where are you going to?"

The only one that spoke Egyptian was Laurence. "We are children of the many nations and we are on a peace mission, for our people fear the great King Shishok. We are on our way to offer our peoples respect and hope to form an alliance"

"The pharaoh is on his way back to Tanis and more than likely reached there by now," said the guard. "I know one way that you could help the King. If you could do this while you are on your way to see him."

"Tell me what that would be then, I beg of you," answered Laurence?

"Oh this is an easy one," replied the guard. "Be on the lookout for a small group of Hebrew men, we rode with the pharaoh as we conquered all of their cities and cut down their King!"

"That is easy," stated Laurence.

"Well then, may the Gods favor your journey" Laurence told the guard.

Adsideo and the others waved to the Egyptians as they turned and began walking towards the camp. As the Egyptians rode off there was a sudden gust of wind that blew their headdresses, and before their eyes the Egyptians were disintegrated into a sand storm of small but powerful burst that only lasted a matter of seconds! To their astonishment nothing of the Egyptians remained.

"Lets load up and get out of here before God has to raise the desert floor level any more" said Sylvester.

After that they mounted and rode hard while still carrying the Ark on the two mules.

They were able to move a little faster though it was not fast enough for Democritus. He was ready to get this over with and head back to Sestus. It would be fall in a couple of months and he had a woman and a place to spend it. He wondered if they were as nervous about the task ahead as he was. What had God meant when he said they would be rewarded. Had they all had other plans besides returning to the temple? He pondered on this for a few minutes when, Maurice started speaking about Arsinoe, the city they were approaching. For he said he knew this place too well. It was a crap hole and a villainous place.

"Everyone watch each other at all times" he said to all of them. He was very serious it seemed.

"This place will eat us up and then deliver us to Shishok. I would suggest that we stay together and not stall for long at all."

Maurice went on, "there is a well at the northwest corner of the city, but we will have to enter through the gated area, so please keep your eyes open!"

"All right everyone," said Adsideo "we need to listen to Maurice on this one, this is his country and I expect no single minded actions. Please listen and watch what is going on. You are all aware of what would happen if the Ark fell into the wrong hands," he added.

Dominic said "they may not know what would happen, but if you ever have time I could tell you all about it".

"Let's not talk of this yet" added Laurence.

"What is it that you mean to hide from the rest of us?" said Arminius.

"Oh he did not mean anything by that" said Colin.

31

"What is the big mystery that looms over this conversation?" Arminius said as he mimicked Laurence.

Adsideo jumped in and said "come, lets put this to rest. If the Ark is carried by anyone other than the Hebrew only bad and evil will rule until all is turned to ash and then eternal darkness will rule over all. The Israelites will not return home. The Ark shall not fall into foreign hands again."

"Well at least we know who to count on when it really comes down to it," said Arminius!

"I hear you little brother," added Sylvester "and what is the big secret about this, all of the civilizations know of the Arks power!"

Adsideo replied, "though it is not a secret, what is a secret will remain a secret and you should all forget about this."

"I will not be told what to forget!" said Arminius.

"Calm down, now are you are ready to go into Arsinoe" said Maurice "as a matter of fact you can go in first.

All right said Arminius "I will wait for your sign before I enter." As they approached the gated area at Arsinoe they could make out someone in the small town scurrying about like the plague was headed their way.

"All right! Did you see that?" said Maurice "yeah, I saw it" said Arminius.

"Ok, watch what I do and do as I do" Maurice said.

As they rode up to the first building, they did not notice the shadow that moved over it. It was as if death was watching them. Adsideo had a bad feeling and Dominic could tell something was wrong.

What was this that was happening to the air? It seemed stagnant, thought Adsideo.

Then suddenly there jumped from the roof and out from behind the building at least ten men.

They were swinging short swords very swiftly.

Just as Sylvester reached the first of the attackers, the enemies vanished before him and fell as sand right at his feet. He turned and saw that the other attackers were gone as well.

The rest of the group was astonished. Even though they had witnessed this the last couple of times, it was not too reassuring that it was so easy to take the life from a man.

Adsideo called out! "Come on, let's get what we came for and be on our way."

As they rode on through the town they could see the well at the end of the main street.

Laurence leaned over and said to Democritus "I have not seen any lights in the windows, nor under the doorways either."

"You are right," said Democritus.

He then rode up quickly to Maurice.

"Stop," said Maurice.

"Something is just not right," he said.

Colin said, "lets turn around, surely we can get water somewhere else"

"There is nowhere else for two days ride" said Maurice.

"Lets get the water and go!" one of the others said.

"All right, Sylvester come with me and we will get the water. The rest of you stay here and guard the Ark.," said Adsideo.

They rode to the well and dismounted from the horses. Adsideo removed the wineskins from the horses as Sylvester walked up to the well. All of a sudden Sylvester yelled to Adsideo "get back, do not come over here"

"What is wrong?" asked Adsideo.

"The well is full of dead bodies," yelled Sylvester "the heads are stacked on top of all of them" he was very upset and there was a scow on his face that showed it.

Adsideo rushed over, leaving the wineskins where he had dropped them, and saw the heads of a woman and two girls.

"Come on. Let us find these animals that did this!" said Sylvester.

"You are right, only animals would do something like this," said Adsideo as he signaled to the others to come ahead.

Maurice and Democritus reached the well ahead of the others and Maurice asked if the water was obtained.

"The well is full of the murdered towns people," said Adsideo.

"Even the children were murdered," added Sylvester.

"Then who did we see as we approached the town earlier" asked Dominic "it sure wasn't the guys that we met at the first corner"

Maurice looked into the well and then reached in and picked up the head of a woman. It was Alyssa, his sister!

He fell down to his knees and cried. Still holding his sisters severed head.

"What were you doing here Alyssa" he said out loud before realizing he had spoken.

"What had she been doing here? She should have been in Pelsium. Axius had told him that she was still running the pottery shop in Pelsium! He had said he spoke with her regularly!"

"God why my sister?" why did she have to die? Why my sister"

"Come on," said Laurence "we must stay here and bury these people"

"After that we are going after those Egyptians that did this," said Colin.

"You are damn right we are" said Arminius "and when we find them..."

"Wait a minute," said Dominic "you cannot expect to use the Ark to avenge these people"

"These were non-believers why should we even bother with burying them?" said Sylvester.

"These were my people, they were not dogs" said Maurice, as he stepped towards Sylvester with his chest bowed up.

Sylvester had been standing with his arms folded he suddenly dropped his arms and began towards Maurice.

"Arminius get between them!" said Adsideo.

As Arminius, Laurence and Colin began towards the two disputed ones, Adsideo dove in between Sylvester and Maurice.

"Break this up, now!" Yelled Dominic "We mustn't fight between ourselves!"

"Come on calm yourselves, Laurence said to Sylvester while looking him in the eye. "he didn't mean anything by it" said Democritus"

"Okay, I am all right," said Maurice "maybe I took it wrong."

Then Maurice said to the others "brothers of the guard, I shall have to take leave from our journey to Sinai, I must avenge my sister"

"I cannot let you go alone, I shall go with you," said Arminius.

"Then I shall ride with you as well," said Sylvester.

"All right then, we shall all go with you," said Adsideo.

After another day and a half of burying the dead of Arsinoe they began to prepare to leave the town. Maurice had all ready scouted the Egyptians exit route and had followed for a couple of hours the day before to make sure it was not a blind trail. He also found a well a few hours ride out of the town and filled his wineskin to show the others that he had found the watering hole.

Once he returned back to meet the others he was convinced that he knew their trail would lead them to the murders.

They left before sunset the next evening. Maurice leading them, followed by Sylvester, Laurence, Adsideo, Democritus, Dominic, Arminius, and Colin at the end. It seems that the Egyptians are headed towards Elath.

Maurice prepared the others for the road ahead of them. It was to be a rough one. The terrain was mountainous and very dangerous. It would be cool during the day in the crevices of the lowlands and hot on the mountainside. Either way it would be cold at night.

They would not be able to make the good traveling time that they were before. And on top of that they were heading the opposite way from Mt. Sinai. There were bandits and low life of every kind hiding through out the mountains. There would also be the Egyptians spies too.

Maurice knew that they would over run the Egyptian army who would be slower than they would be. This could be a good way to ride around them and catch them at one of the passes.

This was a forsaken land, yet it was the birthplace of God's laws to the people.

Chapter Six

The first few days there was not much talk around the camp. Each of them did their duties of cooking, tending the animals, or water detail.

Adsideo, like the others, could not get the citizens of Arsinoe out of his head.

The memory of the looks on the faces of each of the severed heads was the same it seemed. After having to try to match heads with bodies it had left a grief on all of their consciences. They were unable to bury all of the bodies so the wrapped each one in linens or wool and then put aboard ships and set afire in the gulf waters.

On the fifth day there was signs that they were closing in on them. They came upon a camp that had fires that were still smoldering and some of the tents had been left standing. It seemed that they might have seen the Templars approaching and had been in a hurry to leave.

Had they been afraid? Were they surprised by something? Why would they leave so quickly? Maybe they saw someone or something and pursued after it.

Maurice noticed that there were camel tracks all around the camp. A lot of them too. Maybe the locals had surprised the Egyptians and they had to scatter or had pursued after the attackers.

This was doubtful since there was not a sign of a fight.

Now this camp was at the foot of two mountains that feed into a valley and from the tracks they lead into the valley.

Maurice said, "let us ride into the valley and see where it will lead us to the murdering bastards"

Now the others have heard Maurice's plan to cut off the Egyptian army in such a valley and was leery of this for they were afraid of the same thing happening to them.

Arminius was the first to speak up "I do not like this he said, what if they are awaiting us. They could have seen us coming from a scouts perch on the mountainside".

"Do not worry, I do not think that they would have up and run from us like that. They would have stood and fought us," replied Maurice.

"He is right," said Adsideo" there are only eight of us"

Democritus said "but what if they heard some how about the destruction of the others by the Ark or some how heard of the power of the Ark"

"That is a possibility," said Dominic.

"Let us unload the Ark and carry it thought the valley pass," said Colin.

Adsideo said "we do not know that this would be the will of God to strike down the enemy of the non-believers"

Maurice added, "You forget my friend that they are the ones that struck down King Rehoboam and our army as well, then plundered the temple"

"Yes, but as we all know from the voice of God that this was his will," said Adsideo.

"Let us stop this bickering," said Sylvester.

"Let us decide by a vote" said Democritus "weather or not to ride into the valley with or without the Ark being carried by man or by beast"

"This sounds fair to me" seconded Arminius.

All of the others agreed with Dominic that they would carry the Ark though the valley in case of a surprise.

There was a cavern near this place that they harbored the mules and six of the horses. Dominic and Laurence were to ride and the rest would carry the Ark it was decided.

They ate and rested for an hour or so and within that time they discussed the journey ahead and the events of the past several weeks.

They all were brothers of one extended family it seemed to Adsideo and he could see on the faces of the others at that time that this held true to the others as well.

He saw that there was a great comfort and love with the actions of the others as they spoke with each other of the acts they had witnessed.

Some how he knew that they were all part of a special group of bothers that was destined to succeed in their mission from God himself.

"Everyone ready for a journey to our destiny?" said Arminius.

"Aye" said Colin.

Adsideo said to the others "as we prepare for the unknown ahead let us see it in our hearts to see after the Ark and each other, to see in our minds the arm and justice of our lord God, and may he watch over us. Brothers let us go with the will of God at our side".

As they took up the Ark there was a sudden gust of the wind and it set itself before them as a cyclone of dust.

"This is a very good sign," said Dominic.

They traveled into the valley and continued on the trail of the Egyptians throughout the day. As the sun began to drop below the mountains they camped in a place of the valley that they had come up on that forked into another crevice in the mountain. This crevice was a dead-end so they camped at the mouth of it so not to be trapped.

Laurence had snared a couple of rabbits with the aid of Maurice before the sun had set and they prepared this for meal that night.

As they sat and ate that night they spoke of the journey to the mountains and how different it was compared to the journey along the coastline that they had followed to Pelusuim.

Maurice described to them his youth and how it had led him to this place once before under the King of Pelusuim. They had come to take back the daughter of the King from kidnappers who had taken her from her room in her father's palace.

It was Edommites that had conspired to this kidnapping and it turned into a war before they could complete the mission.

The Princess was returned to the army of Pelusuim in time, but she had been driven mad by repeated rape and starvation.

This had not turned out to be the healthy thing for the Edommites who were punished very harshly.

The Pelusuimities took every man, women, and child into slavery as they were still in captivity to this day.

During this campaign for the King's daughter they had passed through this very valley floor. If Maurice could remember right there was an open plain about half of a days ride toward the east. They spoke of this and decided that they would continue on through the valley and then take the southern route though the open plain until they reached AElana.

The next morning they continued on their pursuit of the Egyptians and make good time.

They reached the open plain of Paran before midday and headed southeasterly toward AElana.

Shortly afternoon Maurice pointed out that they could see the Egyptians ahead in the distance.

They stopped for a short break and discussed their next move.

Sylvester recommended that Dominic and Laurence should ride ahead and get the Egyptians to stop.

"No this will not work," said Adsideo "it would be to dangerous for them alone"

"Look!" shouted Democritus "they have seen us, and are headed back towards us"

"Then our questions have been answered by the Lord once again," stated Dominic.

"All right everyone watch each others backs!" said Adsideo.

"What do you think? Laurence said to Arminius "is this a good day to seek battle?"

"Any day is as good as the other for a chance to meet your maker" replied Arminius.

"Well, just do not make it today" said Adsideo "for we still have another agenda to fill"

As the Egyptians were still a good half an hour away they prepared the Ark for battle in hopes that God would not find their vengeance unworthy.

"Dominic say a prayer for us and make an offering" said Colin.

"I will not be able to sacrifice here but I will ask for forgiveness for us." Dominic replied.

"I have some anointing oil if you would like to be blessed" he added.

"All of you bow in a line and I will anoint you before battle." Dominic told the others.

They all did as they were asked and Dominic raised the oil in front of Colin first and said "God, if you find it in your hearts today for vengeance of the unblessed but deserving dead of Arsinoe then make it so, in your name we pray" and he splashed the anointing oil over the hair and shoulders of Colin.

Next he did the same to the next in line, which was Adsideo, followed by Sylvester, Democritus, Maurice, Laurence, and last in line was Arminius.

He continued after Adsideo to Sylvester and as he did so, Adsideo could see that there was a tide of sand rising in between them and the Egyptians. It rose up approx. 40

cubits high and seemed to stand in place. The Egyptians kept on coming as though they did not see it!

Suddenly it rushed towards the Egyptians and they were washed away by it as though it was the sea swallowing them never to be seen again.

"They are all gone," whispered Laurence.

"Yes, it is done," said Maurice.

"Well, let us not dwell on this since we did not have but a hand in this. It has been the work of God himself," said Dominic. "Let us pay no homage to them"

So they turned back towards the valley and headed back to the cavern. They stopped at the mouth of the valley at the request of Dominic and another prayer was said to God for the safety and blessing of all.

They reached the cavern the morning after that and laid down for some rest as Maurice hunted up some hens for dinner. He also found some pomegranates and picked a couple for each of the others as well as himself.

When he reached the cavern he could see that all was well and the others were fast asleep except for Adsideo who was sitting at the opening in the rocky hillside.

"Why are you not resting like as the others?" asked Maurice.

"I could not sleep," said Adsideo.

"Would you help me prepare for the meal? Asked Maurice.

"Of course" replied Adsideo "I do have to say that I am not much of a cook" he said.

"That is all right," said Maurice "you can learn"

"Once we complete this meal you should get some rest Adsideo," said Maurice said to him.

"I am not the one who was out in the heat hunting!" Adsideo said, "you rest and I think I can manage to cook a couple of prairie birds"

"I will take you up on that then brother" Maurice replied.

"You sleep and I will wake all of you when it is ready" said Adsideo.

Adsideo completed the preparations for the food and then woke the others.

"The smell of food is the greatest thing to wake up to," said Sylvester.

"I agree with that statement" seconded Arminius.

"Well you men enjoy, I must sleep before I fall over in front of all of you" said Adsideo as he walked towards the corner of the cavern with his bedroll.

The others tended to the horses and cleaned up after the cooks.

Once asleep Adsideo began to dream. He dreamed that he was sitting at the fire in the center of the cave. He was alone.

Then all of a sudden there was a crevasse that opened into the cave that began to pour out light. The light was so bright that he could not look at it. It filled him with a feeling of sudden love and joy. He felt very safe but yet he laid his face to the ground as if to hide.

"Adsideo, rise!" said a voice. This was not the voice he had heard in the tabernacle in Jerusalem. When he looked up he saw the image of a man.

He was just standing there in front of Adsideo at first. There was something about the appearance of this man. He seemed to have an aurora around him that was noticeably tinted in a blue light.

He slowly turned his back to Adsideo and began to walk towards the rear wall of the cave.

When Adsideo and the others had first entered the cave to stable the animals he had noticed that there. Were sconces cut into the wall face and there was oil in these that was lit as lamps. This was not unusual for any cave, in this part of the world or any other part of the world, which the others may have used for shelter.

As the man reached the rear wall he reached into one of the lit cups and suddenly there opened a hidden passage.

Adsideo rose up and watched as the man walked into the passage. Adsideo followed only to discover that though the passage remained open the man had vanished!

Just inside the passage there was a torch sconce, which Adsideo removed the torch from and began to walk down the corridor. It was wide enough for a horse and cart to be ridden through and had been carved smooth by some means that Adsideo had never seen before. The walls were possibly carved by water or some other means unknown to Adsideo and any other speculation was just that.

He continued though the corridor until he came to a "T" shaped junction. Some how he felt that he should turn to the left and did so. Once around the corner he saw that the passage began to slope downwards at a gentle slope. Downwards he continued into the blackness of the passageway until he came to a very large cavern room. He noticed that there were torch sconces on his side of the cavern walls and he found a torch to light and installed it in one of the sconces. He also saw that there were more of them as he walked along.

As the light grew in the room he saw that there was a large map engraved into the far wall.

He began to approach the wall. He could see that it was quite intricately carved in great detail. This seemed to be a map of the corridor he had followed and they seemed to go on for a very long ways.

He looked at the map for what felt like a very long time.

Suddenly Adsideo awoke from the dream and sat up very quickly! He was sweating and was very thirsty.

Laurence came over to him and said to him "What is wrong? Did you have a bad dream"?

"No" replied Adsideo "it may have. Been a good dream"

Chapter Seven

Adsideo stood up and went over to a water bowl that had been filled by Colin and washed his face.

As he looked up he saw the wall sconce that the man in his dream had touched to open the passage. He began towards it and stuck his hand out to grab the sconce and noticed that there was a peg sticking out of the wall right inside the wall sconce. He touched it and the wall opened as in the dream!

"How did you know where that switch was?" asked Maurice "I thought you had never been this far south before"

"I have not been here before, I saw this in the dream I just awoke from" replied Adsideo.

"Lets get the animals packed, we are leaving here," said Adsideo.

"What are you talking about"? Asked Laurence.

"Do as I say, quickly" said Adsideo firmly this time.

"Hey now, he did know about the switch that opened the doorway" said Arminius.

"That is proof enough for me" added Dominic.

Adsideo began to walk through the opening and signaled for the others to follow him.

Sylvester said "Hey, Adsideo allow me to go ahead of you. If anyone is waiting on us I will be the first onto the trap."

"No it will be all right, I went further than this into the tunnels in my dream" said Adsideo.

"What if it is not all like the dream," asked Dominic.

"Allow us to know about your dream before we go with you" said Colin.

"Just come on and quit asking questions until we reach the map room ahead then I will tell you every thing I saw in my dream" said Adsideo as he looked at the others with such confidence that they knew he felt very strong about this matter.

"Well lead the way my good man" said Democritus.

"The map room huh? Added Arminius.

Adsideo began into the wide corridor as the others followed him. Arminius and Colin were leading the mules with the horses tied one to the other behind the rest of them. The Ark was taken from the pack animals and carried by Maurice, Laurence, Democritus, and Sylvester. Dominic followed behind Adsideo.

They reached the "T" hallway rather quickly and began to descend down the pathway.

Once Adsideo turned the corner he could see that there was light ahead. Once they reached the map room Adsideo could only then in the light see how large this room was. He could see that all of the torches were lit. There were at least seventy five to one hundred torches lining the round room. There was column after column in the center area of the room that was carved out of the stone foundation of the mountain. Around the outside of the column rows their was a circular pathway that was very wide and from the entry that Adsideo had taken into this room in his dream he did not even see the columns, but now in the light he was amazed at it's size.

Adsideo led the others to the opposite side of the room and stood in front of the map. It was just as it had been in the dream other than now it seemed much more clear and even more intricate than before.

The others gathered around the map in amazement! "It looks as if this goes a long way beneath the surface," said Dominic.

"I wonder who made these tunnels?" said Arminius.

"Look here, the map appears to marked by a burning tree at the center," said Colin.

"If I was to guess, I would say that this is probably the burning bush of Mt. Sinai" said Dominic.

"Could it be" asked Democritus "should we be so lucky as to find a safe passage to the Lord's home"

"I do not believe it is luck," said Adsideo "it was only a very short while ago that I was shown this by a man in my dream"

"Tell us about the dream" said Sylvester "I would like to hear this"

Adsideo told all of them in great detail about the man in the dream and the dream it's self.

After he had finished telling his tale Arminius spoke up. "I had a dream when we were camped in the wilderness outside of Pelusuim" said Arminius. "I was in a cavern much like this room except a lot different features. There was a fountain in the middle of the room and on the other side a throne of gold and may other furnishings of gold as well. Behind the throne was tapestries woven of gold thread"

"This is very interesting," said Adsideo "two of us with nearly the same dream"

"I think this is another intervention by the Lord to lead us safely to the mountain as he told us to bring the Ark to in the beginning of our journey." Said Laurence.

"I hope you are all right about this," said Arminius.

"How are we to feed ourselves and the animals, and what about water" said Sylvester.

"I think this is one of those times that we were taught before to have a little faith," said Dominic rather sharply.

"What do you mean by that?" said Sylvester.

"Exactly what it sounded like, have some backbone you wild heathen!" said Dominic.

"Hold it! Hold it right there" said Maurice "we will not begin fighting amongst ourselves!"

Maurice continued to speak as he turned to Dominic "now that was uncalled for!" why did you speak to Sylvester like that, he is one of us and we made a pact a long time ago. The Templar guard will always stand together!"

"I do not know what made me say these things," said Dominic, his right eyebrow raised as he extended his hand towards Sylvester "I apologize with the utmost respect to you and your kind"

"That is all right," said Sylvester "I know now that you are sincere"

They shook hands as the others looked at each other strangely.

They continued to look at and study the map as a group. "How are we supposed to memorize this map?" said Democritus "there are thousands of tunnels and doorways marked here"

"Look at this corridor that leads out of the other side of this room" said Adsideo he followed its path with his finger and showed the others how it lead all the way to the mountain marked by the burning bush.

"Alright lets search the rest of this room and then we will see if we can find something to copy the map with," said Colin.

"We need something to draw on" said Adsideo "and look for any supplies that we might be able to use as well"

They spread out in groups of two and began to search this room. It was approx. 60,000 square cubits, though this was only an estimate. By Adsideo' s recollection.

Adsideo and Sylvester searched the southern side, Dominic and Maurice the eastern side, Democritus and Laurence the western side, which was the map wall, and

Colin and Arminius the northern sections. They had agreed to meet in the center of the room.

Now as they began the search Adsideo noticed that the walls had glyphs carved into them and were of a strange origin, one he had never seen before. They looked very, very old. There was a carving of an army at the scene of a battle being fought, and of what appeared to be a crest of nobility carved in the stone above the glyphs. The soldiers and the nobles had great headdresses of feathers and helmets forged of metal. These were very strange since the only peoples he had ever seen of such stature had been the Egyptians. These he knew were not Egyptian's. As he looked at them he thought that he saw some movement in one of the carved faces! "Hey did you see that?" said Adsideo to Sylvester.

"See what?" Replied Sylvester.

Then Adsideo discarded this due to the lighting in the room. "Nothing, I thought one of the faces turned to look at me once I passed it" said Adsideo.

"Well if you are trying to scare me, it will not work. I am not scared easily," said Sylvester "but if you see it again let me know"

"I will keep that in mind" said Adsideo.

"Now that you say these things, I feel as though I am being watched by someone," said Sylvester.

"Do not worry, it could have been my imagination" said Adsideo. "I have been known to be wrong you know"

Colin and Arminius found the northern area and began their search. Like Adsideo and Sylvester they noticed the wall carvings and began to look at them in detail.

Colin said "I have never seen such horrible looking soldiers before these ungodly men in the carving. Some of them look more like winged demons and beasts"

"Do not worry about what has been" said Arminius.

"Where did you get this piece of advice?" said Colin.

"I do not know, it just seemed to come out," said Arminius.

'Hey look over there" said Arminius "it looks to be a chest of some kind"

"Be careful not to open it to quickly," said Colin "lets look at it first. Let us make sure there are not any traps of any kind"

Colin began to walk over to the chest and it began to open on it's own!

"Step back from it," said Arminius "something is moving in the wall carvings, get away from there!"

Suddenly it opened slightly and Colin stepped back a step, he could see inside of it through the cracked opening.

There appeared to be jewels and pearls in it! He could see golden objects also!

"Do not touch any of those items Colin!" said Arminius suddenly.

"We are rich men now" said Colin "what do you mean, do not touch it?" asked Colin as he walked closer to the chest.

"Nooo!" said Arminius as he pushed Colin to the ground. "Stay down, this is a trap I know it is!" said Arminius.

"Maurice, slow down a little" said Dominic "I am not as young as I used to be"

"Just keep behind me a little," said Maurice.

"It's hard to keep up a conversation if you are not at least a little closer" said Dominic.

"We do not need conversation right now," replied Maurice "what we need is to complete this search and meet back with the others as soon as possible"

"Just stay back behind me, I will lead" Maurice reiterated to Dominic.

"Make sure you do not lead us into a dead end" said Dominic.

"You talk to much, be quite," said Maurice.

Maurice was coming up to the northeastern wall. Maurice glanced at the wall carvings for a moment but did not pay any attention to the army of soldiers carved in the walls. They would turn to their left and begin the search of the eastern corridor between the columns and the east wall. Down at the mid-section of this wall there seemed to be a door casing. "Just as on the map" said Maurice "I would bet that this is the corridor leading to Mt. Sinai"

"After what I have seen over the last few hours I would agree," said Dominic.

They continued on towards the door casing. There were Cherub statues at either side of the door casing holding long pikes with oil lamps on top of them and they were lit as well as the torches that lined the walls and one each side of the columns that lined their left side. They walked up to the statues and then between them to look at the door. What a surprise to Dominic, the doors that looked just like the ones at the tabernacle in Jerusalem!

Democritus studied the map and was tracing back and forth from this room, which was marked on the map, to the mountain that was marked with the burning bush symbol.

Laurence had been searching around the columns and had not found anything to write on or with for that matter.

"Are you going to help me or what?" said Laurence "I would think that you would have that map all memorized by now!"

Democritus replied by saying "I would rather that we find something to copy our route with in case something was to happen to me, I guess I had better help you search"

"That would be nice," murmured Laurence.

They began to look towards the corners and on either side of the columns.

Laurence began looking at the piles of furnishings, which were stacked against the wall.

There was a painting on wood framed animal hide that showed a harem of concubines that caught his eye. They were all very well dressed and ornamented.

They must have belonged to a very wealthy man thought Laurence to himself as he looked at the painting.

"Hey come and look at this," said Laurence "it is some kind of drawing of whores, painted on a frame"

"I am not looking for whores right now" said Democritus replied without looking back to Laurence. He continued to search the far corner.

Laurence could not take his eyes off of the painting. He was very pleased by one of the figures in the drawing. Suddenly she turned from her profile and held up her hand and blew a kiss to Laurence!

"Come here and look at this," said Laurence as he kept staring at the painting.

Adsideo and Sylvester continued to walk between the wall of hieroglyphics and column rows. Adsideo noticed in the carvings that there was a scene of a great King sitting on a throne and he was pointing down to a kneeling man before him. There was a Queen sitting next to this mighty King. It was the man he had seen in his dream. The one who showed him the switch to the door? Sitting down on either side of them was an enrage' of handmaidens, guards, and advisors. Down the steps from this sitting King there were dancers and acrobats. There were both male and female and were in rows of same sex facing the opposite sex. The females were either holding there hands in the air or bowing to the males. The males were all excepting the flirtations of the females in different ways.

They were magnificent and were carved in such detail. Adsideo could not believe the detail. The King mesmerized him.

"Hey, look over here there is the crest of the guard on these soldier's armor and shields. It is the same crest of the Templars. How could that be, you designed this crest yourself Adsideo, I saw you when you drew it the first time" Sylvester said.

Adsideo looked over to where Sylvester pointed and looked at the crest on the shields.

"I did design this after a dream I had the night before drawing it and getting the approval of King Solomon the very next day" said Adsideo.

Suddenly there was a bolt of green dust that came forward and hit Sylvester right in the forehead. He slumped to the ground so fast that his body fell to the ground like it was a lifeless mass of flesh.

"Look at me," said a strange voice. Adsideo looked around behind him and there, in the carving. He saw that the King was now standing and walking towards him. The handmaidens were fanning him as he walked towards Adsideo.

"We are the guard of the past, we, like you, were delivered by God to serve God and his chosen ones" said the King "the others of your group are in danger of this room. This is the room of temptation, and should only be entered by those expecting the tests and trails. None of the unsuspecting candidates have ever made the trials" he continued to walk towards Adsideo but kept within the context of the wall surface.

"What do you mean trials? Who are you? How do you speak to me?" asked Adsideo "what type of sorcery is this?

"What you are now witnessing is not sorcery, it will prove to be a blessing if you heed my warnings" replied the King "now in this room lives another, besides me" "he is on the other side of this room and can be found trapped in the wall like I am." "He is very evil and will lead mankind to darkness, despair, and disaster. I and my soldiers are locked in an eternal war with their evil kind" "this war is fought here daily as is it fought in the minds of good and evil men elsewhere in the world"

"Find your men and leave this room as soon as possible.

Exit to the Eastern wall of Hope. This is where your journey will begin!" said the King as he pointed toward the eastern wall, which was to his right side.

"First you must find your brothers and what ever you do not take the Ark to the north wall or the deceptive ones will take it from you and all hope will be lost. There will only be despair and darkness!" "Darkness will once again rule the world, God will forsake mankind and eventually destroy the earth by a flood but unlike the last one that formed these very corridors this one will be of fire"

"Hurry, Adsideo! Do not tell the others about my warnings and me until the time is right. This is your trial, so be prepared"

Sylvester began to stir and groaned.

As he sat up.

"What happened? Why am I on the floor?"

"You hit your head you clumsy fool" said Adsideo "now hurry and help me find the others, there is danger here we must find them and leave this place"

"What are you talking about? This place is as safe as it will ever get," said Sylvester.

"If only you knew how wrong you are right now, but there is no time for this!" said Adsideo "lets find the others now and then I may explain this to you later"

"Let us get back to the map wall and help Democritus and Laurence with the Ark and then we will find the others" said Adsideo.

"Get off of me," said Colin to Arminius "what has gotten into you"

"The carving's, look at them" said Arminius "they all moved their eyes and one of them smiled as you began toward the chest"

"Have you gone mad? They are made of stone!" Said Colin.

"Look at them now" said Arminius.

The dark army began at that moment to move and the leader, or general of the troops rode a chariot over to the front lower section of the wall carving. He began to speak to the two Templar Guards as they sat up and watched with dismay.

"Bring me the Ark and you shall live as the richest of Kings from now until the end of eternity," said the dark voice.

"I am Bellabezzer, the dark one. Commander of the true God's army. I will make a place for you in the masters halls where you will forever live."

The two stood and were mesmerized by the General's speech. They began to walk closer to the wall carving, never once looking at each other or in any direction except at the General's face.

The General was wearing a suit of Armour with the crest of a winged demon on his chest. His helmet was covering all of his face with the exception of his eye's, which now glowed a fiery red. His armor seemed to be alive with different faces of agony that moved in random patterns and each cried out in pain as he spoke.

"Bring the Ark to me, now!" said Bellabezzer.

Suddenly Arminius shook his head for a vision of the others came into his mind. "Get away from us!" he shouted at the General.

With a quick shove he pushed Colin to the ground again!

"Do not listen to him Colin," said Arminius "let us leave here now!"

Colin fell to the ground and quickly rolled on his shoulder and the rose up and rushed at Arminius.

"I will kill you!" he said in a voice not of his own.

He rushed at Arminius and grabbed his head, gouging at his eyes. Arminius fought back and again pushed Colin to the ground. This time he leaped on top of him and held him down.

As they rolled Bellabezzer's arm lunged out of the wall and came within inches of grabbing Arminius by his long red hair. A scream of anguish came from Bellabezzer and at the same time from the lost souls in his armor.

Arminius and Colin continued to scuffle on the ground when very quickly Arminius rolled over on top of Colin and began to strike him in the face with his fist.

As he was hitting Colin he was yelling with each blow to Colin's head. "I will not allow this of you! You will come with me away from this evil one"

Colin rolled out from under Arminius and sprang up and ran towards the eastern corner. Arminius followed behind him and tackled him at the corner. They began to wrestle on the ground again and Colin said "I am listening to you, do not strike me any more!"

As he said this Bellabezzer's horse and chariot could be heard coming towards them as if it was on the very ground that they lie upon! As he rode towards them he had a pike stuck out through the wall and was about to jab it into Arminius when he and Colin rolled away from the wall just enough to avoid the blow. Once again the harrowing screams came from the Dark Lord and his suit of armor.

Arminius pulled Colin to his feet and they ran towards the south along the eastern corridor. They could make out the two figures of Maurice and Dominic ahead in the distance.

As they ran up to Maurice, Arminius said, "run away as fast as you can!"

"What are you running from?" asked Maurice.

"The evil army of Bellabezzer, they are coming for us all and they want the Ark," said Arminius Colin shook his head as if to agree with his companion.

"Look, there is no one here but us," said Dominic.

Arminius and Colin turned in between the cherub statues and looked back towards the northern wall. They were looking between the cherub's stone legs.

"He is coming I tell you" said Colin "he almost had us twice"

"Let us find the others at the center of the room as we agreed to do," said Arminius "we must warn them and make sure that the Ark is safe"

"All right" said Maurice "we have searched all that there is to be found here"

The four of them walked from the door labeled with the one word "Hope" above its jamb, into the center row of the great columns.

As they walked into the rows of columns Dominic was looking all around he was very leery because of the stories from Arminius as he was telling Maurice what they had seen. Dominic noticed that the ceiling was colored to look like the blue sky. It was slightly painted in wisps of clouds here and there and looked just like a partly cloudy sky. It appeared to be either a sunrise or at sunset since it reflected a dim but beautiful glow to it and was almost as real to him had he not known that they were deep below a mountain.

"Maybe it was the light playing on your minds," said Maurice "I saw the carvings along that wall and they were rather disturbing"

"Disturbing! You would not think they were so disturbing had it tried to kill you," replied Colin.

"Alright I understand you have been spooked. Now calm down and we will be safe together," said Maurice in return to Colin.

"What we saw was real," said Arminius "let us find the others and get the Ark out of this room as soon as possible!"

"Laurence, come to me and take my hand," said the voice of the women "I can leave this place with you if you only take my hand"

Laurence began to stick out his hand when suddenly Adsideo and Sylvester came around the corner.

"Come on, we are leaving now!" said Adsideo "come on Democritus, you and Laurence help us get the Ark and we shall meet with the others"

Democritus began to walk towards the Ark where Sylvester and Adsideo had grabbed on to the lifting poles and prepared to load them back on the mules.

"Laurence, come on" repeated Democritus.

"Do not listen to them," said the women's voice to Laurence "come to me and we will make wonderful lovers"

"Laurence, what has gotten into you? Are you deaf?" said Adsideo "come on we need to go"

All of a sudden as he spoke these words he saw the jeweled arm of a women come through the wall hung painting and she was trying to take Laurence's hand that he had lifted up towards her hand.

Sylvester raised his hand axe quickly and threw it at the women's arm and cut off her hand at the wrist. The hand fell to the ground and burst into flames and was gone with the exception of a jeweled bracelet. Laurence reached down and picked up this bracelet. He looked around and saw that no one noticed as he put it into his pocket.

"Laurence are you alright!" said Sylvester.

"Yes I am alright," said Laurence.

Democritus walked over to Laurence as he back away from the wall painting and noticed that the painting was of a nest of coiled snakes. "I thought you said there were whores in this painting," asked Democritus.

"There were...but now they are gone," replied Laurence.

"Never mind that" said Adsideo "we must be going, the others are in danger"

"Lets go now!" said Sylvester as they picked up the Ark, loaded it on the mules and then grabbed the horses. They headed into the center of the columns.

As they entered the columns there seemed to be sunlight streaming down onto the floor that made the terrazzo glisten and sparkle. Laurence and Sylvester both looked up and saw the clouds and the sun peeping out of these clouds. How could this be they thought for they too knew they were under a mountain. As they continued on they saw a garden area in the center and awaiting their arrival was Maurice, Dominic, Colin, and Arminius.

"Thanks to the Lord, he has protected you and the Ark from this evil place," said Dominic.

"We must leave here at once," said Adsideo "this place is not safe"

"We have found the way out" said Maurice "we found the door out into the corridor. Follow us at once"

As they walked towards the door through the columns they all told their stories with the exception of Adsideo.

"What did you see?" asked Laurence to Adsideo.

"I will tell you all once we are safe and I think I will be allowed too" said Adsideo.

"What did you mean allowed to?" said Democritus.

"No more questions, let us get to the door out of here and be on our way," said Adsideo.

They were soon at the doorway on the eastern wall. Only Maurice, Colin, Arminius, and Dominic had seen the splendor of the cherub statues. The others were in awe of these features to such a dangerous room.

"This is the sign that we have made it though our first trial," said Adsideo.

"For those of us who succeed we shall hold the honor of not only being Knights of the Templar Guard but also Knights of the one true God." Said Adsideo.

They then approached the door and pushed it open rather easily. Out in to the hall they stepped. As they did the doors closed behind them and a locking sound could be heard.

Maurice and Sylvester both turned back and tried to open the massive doors. They were in fact locked and could not be moved.

"We have been closed in to this corridor," said Sylvester.

"It is just the same, it is hopefully safer in here than in there anyways" said Adsideo.

"I will second that," said Arminius.

"Adsideo, you mentioned a minute ago that this completed our first trial? How many trials are there? And what are we being tried for?" said Democritus.

"Wait a minute" said Dominic "who told you we were on trial anyway?"

"I thought we had proven our loyalties to the Lord and the King," said Arminius.

"I know this from being told this inside the room" said Adsideo.

"Well we were told a few things in that room too" said Arminius "and we are not foolish enough to follow them"

"Yes, I was told about the evil one" replied Adsideo "you are wise not to listen to him"

"He said his name was Bellabezzer," said Colin "and he was evil all right"

"He did not have any patience for us either"

"I do trust in the one who told me the things that are good," said Adsideo "he was one of us I can say that"

"Wait a minute, it seems that I remember seeing a crest like ours in the wall carving of the King and his subjects" said Sylvester.

"It will all come back to you in time" said Adsideo.

"How have you known this?" asked Laurence "how do you know that the one that Colin and Arminius saw was not the one to heed to"

"Believe us," said Colin "the one that we saw is not anybody to be listening to"

"Evil I say, he was full of pure hatred if I ever saw it before!" added Arminius.

"I am with Adsideo, what ever he has faith in, so do I" said Sylvester "he is our leader and has been since before this all began"

"That is right," said Maurice "our leader, selected by Solomon himself"

"Hail to the brothers of the Templar," said Dominic "may God bless us all"

"Let us be on our way," said Sylvester.

They walked the horses and pack mules though the corridor and down the sloping pathway.

This corridor was not like the one that had led them to the room of temptation. This one had stone flooring, marble walls and columns, and wall sconce lamps carved in the form of cherubs heads alternating with the heads of some kind of fish head. The fish head sconces had water trickling from their mouths. This water trickled down and under the fish heads, which was collected in a narrow trough of marble and funneled to small bathes that were at every other column row. Each of the bathes had a fountain in it that had the cherubs with their wings folded just like the ones that were on the Ark.

"Let us stop and water the animals," said Adsideo as he climbed down from his horse.

"Do we still have any of the oats for the horses?" asked Maurice.

"There will barely be enough to feed them one last meal," said Democritus.

"Give it all to them tonight" said Adsideo.

"We should save some of it until morning" Laurence said to Adsideo.

"If God intends for us to walk then it will be," replied Adsideo "have faith"

"Things will be alright," Dominic assured the others.

Arminus and Sylvester took the horses over to the pool of water across the corridor on the other side of the room to water them.

"Democritus, where is the next room?" asked Adsideo.

"I did not see any rooms along this corridor on the map. There were four intersecting corridors that join into this one"

"How far to the next corridor would you say?" asked Adsideo.

"We maybe about one-third of the way. It is hard to say, the map did not have any scale or distances marked on it that I could find so I am not sure about the distances"

"Laurence, do we have any food left?" Adsideo asked.

"No, none" replied Laurence.

"Maurice, scout ahead and see if you can find anything to feed us. Democritus go with him," ordered Adsideo.

"Aye" said Democritus as he took his bow and quiver from his horse"

"We will go by foot I suspect," he said to Maurice.

"You would be right in saying that," said Maurice.

"Lead on then friend" said Democritus.

"Do not go to far away, we should all get some rest soon. Each of us will need to stand guard duty in a place like this," said Adsideo.

"We will not be long if my hunting skills are anything to show of," said Maurice.

"We shall see about "your" hunting skills my friend" Democritus mocked Maurice.

"I would like to say," said Sylvester "That the first to bring me a meal will be declared the winner of this contest, for I am very hungry"

"We shall call this the feast of Sylvester," quipped Laurence with a smile.

"Be off with you then" said Dominic "all of this talk has made me hungry"

Arminius had completed the watering and feeding the horses and went over and sat on the edge of the fountain.

Adsideo was telling Maurice again not to take long, once again, as Democritus began walking off down the shadowy corridor followed by Maurice.

Laurence and Dominic went over to begin to remove the straps that held the Ark on the mules.

"We will need a hand with the Ark," said Dominic.

Adsideo, Arminius, Colin, and Sylvester began to walk to the mules.

Adsideo and Sylvester inserted the poles from one end and Laurence and Colin took the other ends of the poles.

They lifted together and walked over to the center column. They sat it down on the floor and removed the covering from it.

As soon as the covering was removed, the Ark began to sparkle and the Lord spoke.

"You and your brethren shall not hunger in the service of the Lord"

"Walk the path laid out before ye, walk the path of faith!"

"Doubt and blindness are on the wayside for those true in heart and full in stomach"

The Ark returned to its golden luster and the Lord spoke no more.

Suddenly throughout the corridor was the smell of fresh baked bread, cheese, and meat roasting on a fire.

Maurice came walking up and said to the others "come brothers, there is a camp set up with cooking food just ahead!"

"Come on Democritus will need our help with all of the food that we saw. Someone else is in this corridor and has prepared a meal for us. And I believe from the way that it smells that it is going to be a very good meal.

"How far away is this camp from where we are now?" asked Adsideo.

"Not far at all" said Maurice "Dominic you and Laurence, take the horses and lead them to the camp that has been supplied for us. The rest of us will bring the Ark," said Adsideo.

It was a quarter of an hour by foot for Adsideo and the others to reach the camp.

Once they reached the camp Democritus, Laurence, Maurice, and Dominic were peering over the food that was prepared for them.

"There was something very strange about this camp site I noticed, once we arrived at it" said Maurice.

"There were no footprints anywhere around the camp"

"Didn't Dominic or Laurence tell you about the message from God or the Ark beginning to sparkle." Asked Adsideo.

"No, I guess their stomachs spoke louder than their memories," laughed Maurice.

Adsideo told Maurice and Democritus about the message from God and how the food was prepared for them though an act of faith.

Chapter Eight

Even as Adsideo sat in his home, looking down at the Chinese man, down towards Geary Street in present time, he could remember that night very well. They all drank wine, ate lamb, and most of them laughed as brothers. It was not until years later that he would look back at this moment and remember that one of them had not laughed along with the rest of them. For this one member of the Templars had already been infected with the lore for power. At that time it went unnoticed.

They held a vote per Democritus's advice and decided that Colin and Dominic would stand the first watch that night in the cavern corridor.

Colin took the west end of the corridor, which they had entered the room from, and Dominic the east end of the corridor. Colin sat and he leaned on the closest of the water fountains.

As Arminius laid there the sound of the water coming from the fish head sconces and the fountains quickly put him to sleep. He quickly began to dream.

In his dream there was a great round room of marble floors and walls. There were four sets of doors, which were opened. Each had a different carving of men in Armour. He walked closer to one of the doorways and the doors closed in front of him before he could reach the portal.

The carving on the door began to speak to him and said, "You must face each of the trials in the given order. Each must be faced without lack of faith, trust, and honor."

"Who are you and where am I?" asked Arminius.

The solider turned back to his carved self and did not reply. Arminius turned and began to run towards the doorway opposite the one he had been at and again the doors closed before he reached them.

"You must heed the warnings and face your trials in the order given to you," said the figure carved in this set of doors.

Arminius then ran to the set of doors to his right-hand and to his surprise they did not close and he ran right into the next room. He stopped in his tracks. Surprised to have been allowed to enter this room.

This room was a very long hall and as he entered it he saw that either side had statues and carvings of many different idols, Gods and Goddess's. There were ones that he had seen before from his travels and others he did not recognize.

He began to slowly walk towards the opposite end of the hallway and stared at the statues as he did so. Looking from one side and back to the other again.

As he walked forward and passed the first couple of these idols he could hear choruses of voices in different languages. They all were calling his name. He began to walk faster, and faster, and faster. Then he was running. He could begin to see the other end of the corridor and there in the end wall were the doors from the tabernacle with the carvings of palm trees, open flowers, and cherubs.

Up ahead of him he began to see that the idols of stone were beginning to move and walk out into the isle. He dodged the first, which had many sets of arms and a huge headdress. The next was the Egyptian God of death Nubius; with his large jackal head he snapped at Arminius and then jumped into the crouch of a canine and snapped again. This time narrowly missing Arminius. He did not look back and kept on running towards the end wall. There ahead of him was a large serpent that towered over Arminius.

Arminius ran right at this huge viper and lunged over the top of its back when its tail slapped him to the ground. It quickly wrapped its self around Arminius and began to squeeze him. He was able to pull his dagger from its sheath just above his sandaled foot. He tried to stab it but as the serpent squeezed him again he dropped the dagger and heard it hit the floor.

Arminius struggled to keep his head above the snakes belly when suddenly he was able to pull his right arm free and pulled his sword from its scabbard. He then thrust it deep into the serpents belly and it released him onto the floor. He then jumped onto the monster again and this time he pushed his sword into one of the eyes of the great snake. It pulled the sword from Arminius' s hand as it began to scream a horrible scream and swung its self uncontrollably about the room. At last it fell lifelessly to the floor.

Arminius then ran over to the serpent and pulled his sword as he continued to run towards the golden doors.

Then jumping out in front of him was the figure of a woman dressed in a loose fitting tunic of pure white silk. As she turned back to look at Arminius he could tell that half of her was white and the other half was black! She was divided in half right down the bridge of her nose and the rest of the way down as well.

She spoke to Arminius and said "Arminius, it is me Hel. Goddess to your people as taught to you as a child. Do not disregard your people! Do not shame your family Arminius"

As Arminius began to run towards her and looking her in the eyes he said "there is only one true God and he will not tolerate false idols like you" he then ran between her legs and continued on to the golden doors of the tabernacle.

Hel turned towards Arminius and said "then you shall come to your death and forever live in my hall of the underworld" then there was a great blast of wind that swept

Arminius off of his feet and rolled him backwards toward the great stone statue of the Goddess.

Into her hands he fell and as she secured her grip around his armored body. She lifted him toward her face and said to him. "You shall soon come to love the pain I will now inflict upon your worthless self"

She then tossed him into the air and maneuvered her head and mouth as she intended to eat him. As Arminius fell he saw her mouth open and pulled his sword. He twisted around in the air as he fell. To his surprise he landed on his feet stratling her lips. As she began to close her mouth she turned her head forward and tilted him off balance. He fell backwards and landed on her tongue. She quickly tried to pull him into her mouth and caused Arminius to loose his sword. As his sword fell he quickly grabbed it. He began to fall forward he thrust it into the chest of the Goddess. He held on to the sword and as the weight of his body pulled downward causing the wound to open up into a great slit, cutting through the stone figure as if it were live flesh. He then fell to the ground.

The Goddess began to fall forward as He began to run so fast from her that he slipped and fell. He then pulled himself up to his feet and he continued to run towards the doors never once looking back. He could see the doors were beginning to open and a bright light was beginning to shine out into the great hall. Stepping out between him and this light he began to see a great many figures of many different shapes and sizes. He began to run even faster towards them with his sword held high and his shield pulled close to his shoulder.

Suddenly Arminius lifted from his sleep and was sitting in the middle of his bedroll with a cold sweat.

"Hey get up, it is your turn to stand watch" said Adsideo whom had taken over for Dominic. Dominic was now fast asleep and laying next to Arminius.

"Adsideo, I just had another of those dreams that have haunted me," said Arminius.

Arminius then told Adsideo and Sylvester, which were the two presently standing, watch.

"Let us keep this between ourselves at this time" said Adsideo "let us not warn the others unless this dream begins to look like the real thing."

"I agree," said Sylvester "no reason to worry the others with dreams"

"Sylvester, awaken Laurence and we too will get some more rest before we continue our journey" Adsideo told Sylvester"

"Will you be able to stand watch" said Adsideo to Arminius.

"Yes, I will be fine now," replied Arminius "maybe even more watchful after my dream"

"Good then, I am tired and will rest" Adsideo said.

Laurence was awake now and picked up some of the bread as he walked to the west side of the camp. Arminius took the eastern side.

Arminius sat upon the rim of the fountain and began to think about the dream. He stared down into the water and wondered what was to happen to all of them.

He began to see the figure of a man mirrored in the water. Arminius turned quickly. He turned to look behind himself. There was no one there behind him as he expected there to be.

"Arminius, look toward me," said a man's voice "I am Aegir of your people. Heed my call to return to the old ways of your fathers before you"

Arminius stood up and backed away from the fountain. "You are not real," said Arminius.

"I am as real as the imaginations of your fathers and of their fathers before them," said Aegir in reply.

"Do not force my anger upon you for I can flood this hall and destroy all of your brethren," said the deity.

71

"You are not the God of my people! I have a new Father," said Arminius very loud.

Laurence began towards Arminius as he heard his yelling.

This awoke the others and they too began towards the fountain. Then suddenly the figure of a man shaped in water. Rose from the water and shot a stream at Arminius and vanished down into the fountain it had came from as Arminius fell down backwards and washed up against the wall.

"What was that?" yelled Laurence "what else lies down that end of the hall"

"It looked like it was some kind of ghost or demon to me," said Maurice.

"It was the image of Aegir the God of the sea from the legends of my people. He began to speak to me from the water in the fountain" said Arminius as he rose back to his feet. He was soaked.

"Let us not make witness to false Gods," said Dominic "we must continued on our way as soon as possible"

"Let us prepare to leave now!" said Adsideo "I have had enough for one evening"

They began to reload the Ark on to the mules and gathered up as much of the food as they could carry on the packs of each horse.

"Arminius, come and speak with me," said Adsideo.

"Yes, did you need me?" asked Arminius as he stood in front of Adsideo.

"Have you been swayed by your faith? After all we have seen together now and in the past," asked Adsideo.

"No, why do you ask this?" said Arminius.

"I was wondering why after all of the others come from other faiths originally and only your faith would conjure itself in front of the others" replied Adsideo.

"Adsideo, are you accusing me of having a lack of faith? Said Arminius quite angered by Adsideo' s remarks.

"I am thinking maybe you are weaker in faith for them to be choosing you instead of the others to try and undermine the goal" said Adsideo.

Arminius began to rush towards Adsideo with his chest bowed out and his arms dancing ahead of the rest of him.

"No one other than God himself shall question my faith in the Lord," yelled Arminius.

"I shall see your death before my own," said Adsideo.

"Stop them," said Sylvester to the others "we must not fight amongst ourselves"

They grabbed Arminius and separated him from Adsideo as the others kept them apart from each other.

"We shall remain as brothers, as Templar Guards, as one," said Dominic.

"Do you not see, that this is a trial?" said Dominic as he turned around slowly in a circle to see the faces of the others. He continued to speak, "do not give in, only the pure of heart and the pure of faith shall succeed. These were the words we all heard together. We should stick together and not fight amongst ourselves"

"I am tired of hearing this same speech by you over and over," said Arminius in such disgust.

"You will all listen to Dominic! For he is our teacher in the faith," said Democritus.

"You need to listen to him," said Sylvester "I will not allow any further disruptions of this kind. Even if I have to tie you to the back of my horse and lead you to the one true God myself" he said as he looked into Arminius' s face.

Arminius began to calm down as the others could be heard talking amongst them selves. They had determined that they should be on there way very quickly and stop any bickering.

They completed loading the animals and began each walking the horses toward the east end of the corridor. The mules were tied to Colin and Arminius' s horses. They made up the rear of the group. Arminius continued to keep his eye on the others as they walked the horses along the corridor. He especially watched Adsideo.

Adsideo heard Sylvester tell Dominic and Laurence of Arminius' dream.

As always Maurice had the lead. Adsideo, Sylvester, Laurence, Dominic, Democritius, Colin, and of course Arminius followed him.

"Be on the lookout for anything suspicious. Keep your heads up and your minds clear," said Adsideo "we shall certainly see more illusions and deceit ahead. I have a feeling this is a long way from over"

As they continued on down the great hall Arminius began to feel isolated by the others. He was thinking about what Hel and Aegir had said about "his people" and about "his fathers" before him.

He began to think about the family that he had once been apart of. The village he grew up in, his mother and father, his siblings. He thought of the fishing and navigational lessons by his father and his uncle. Arminius' s grandfather had died in battle long before Arminius' s birth. There were many legends about Arminius' s grandfather. His name had been Fein of Dago.

Arminius thought of his village and the friends he had there.

He longed to see the coast as he pulled his ship out of port and headed out to the sea.

"Keep your selves tight together with the others" said Maurice "I hear something ahead, and I do not know what it could be. It sounds like rushing water from here."

The corridor began to incline and they were heading up hill now. There was the roar of what did in fact sound to Adsideo as if it was a great river. How could this be he thought to himself. He had heard before of underground rivers but never imagined the sound he was now hearing.

He remembered that once while they had men digging wells for the Temple some of the men had drowned when they had dug through a vein of a subterranean stream or river.

They began to see that there was a sharp bend in the great hall ahead. Adsideo noticed for the first time that the wall sconces were not present at this end of the corridor and it was growing darker now.

As they continued through the bend Adsideo could see a faint light that appeared to be a great distance ahead of them. But it seemed to be getting closer to them at a great speed. It was faster then they were traveling by far.

They rounded the bend in the hall. The roar of rushing water was confirmed by the two big gapping holes through the cavern walls that revealed a rushing river, which gave way to a waterfall that, fell a good 20 cubits. Into another cavern beneath them. There was hardly any water that remained at the bottom of the waterfall. The water ran in to a cavern opening below that was vertical and shaped as a funnel due to the water carving out the rock for an apparently long time.

The corridor they rode through continued on and was carved out over the waterfall. As Adsideo and the others rode towards the waterfall, he could see that where they now rode the walls were hollowed out. You could see through the openings across to the other side of the waterfall. There were half walls formed around the corridor as it wound around another bend in the corridor. This bend was the first that formed a circular hall that went around the waterfall to their left. Adsideo could not believe the view. It truly was breath taking and he thought of this quite often afterwards.

The marble walls and columns had ended as they entered this area. The walls were smooth worn rock walls forming an arch in the center. There were several different colors of stone that appeared to be granite or marble veins. It sparkled as the flames in wall torches flickered.

They continued on around the circular hall Adsideo looked back at the waterfall in awe. Up ahead he saw what appeared to be an opening into another room.

"Watch out, there maybe something ahead," said Maurice.

They began to enter a great room as the one they had seen at the room of temptation. This one also had the forest of columns that consumed the center of the room. It was much larger than the first room but the outer isle were much narrower. All of the outer columns that bordered the corridor were covered in ivy and vine and made the room appear to contain an underground forest. It seemed as if the columns were closer to gather on this outer row of columns and they were fitted with iron fence panels in between each of them. There were also the sounds of birds and other wildlife.

The walls were covered in mosaics of every color and shape of tile. There were representations of every race of man and species of animal. They all seemed to dance together in the largest woodland scene that Adsideo had ever seen.

Adsideo heard the sounds of a cat or possibly another type of animal growling in the tree line, which was but a few cubits away from the fence panels.

"That did not sound friendly," said Laurence.

"There is nothing to worry about, It sounded like a panther or smaller" said Maurice.

"Maybe to you woodsman" said Dominic "I do not like the sound of this place"

"I agree," said Sylvester "and do not forget that we are beneath the surface. How can animals live without sunlight?"

"This is unnatural, we should find the next passage out of here" said Adsideo "Maurice, which way would you recommend?"

"If you believe the map is accurate then we should go to the right," said Democritus.

"I do not remember the waterfalls on the map," said Colin.

"They were there," said Democritus "you just had to look and read between symbols"

"I did not see any trees either," said Dominic sharply as he then smiled trying to promote some humor into this situation.

"Let us follow in Democritus steps," said Maurice "we have to go in some direction"

"Let us get on our way and through this place," said Adsideo "and Dominic you try and be a little more forgiving in your words"

As they turned to there right side and headed to the west now. They could see the mosaic covered wall ahead that was of a pack of wolves attacking deer.

As they rode down this narrow corridor of the column rows they could see how the iron fence fitted between each column was attached. This fence was two to three cubits high and looked to be very strong. The pickets were a hand apart and seemed to be of a square shape with burrs cut into the inside face of each picket.

They could hear the animal sounds within the column rows but other than the mosaics they had not seen any proof of the animals besides the sounds.

77

"Look over there in the far corner" said Maurice "there is a man"

"Where are you looking?" asked Sylvester.

"Ahead of us in the corner of the columns and the fence" replied Maurice.

"I see it," said Colin "it is eating something"

The form came towards them, slowly at first and then it began to pick up it's pace. It was covered either in hair or it was wearing an animal skin of some kind.

"That does not look like a man to me," said Laurence.

"It walks like a man!" said Colin.

"Colin, you and Dominic watch the Ark!" said Adsideo "the rest of us will find out what this creature is"

Maurice and Democritus kicked their horses and began towards the fence ahead of the others. As Adsideo and the others looked on, Maurice and Democritus came upon the creature. It was neither a man nor an animal. It appeared to be both.

"Stay back" said Maurice as his horse reared up and began to whinny.

"I told you this was unnatural," said Adsideo.

The creature stood at the fence it looked at Democritus and at first then it paused, then it screamed and jumped up and down as if to scare him. It appeared to have the face of a human man. A very unshaven and unclean man but a man never the less.

Democritus and Maurice both turned and looked at each other in amazement.

As Adsideo and the others came up behind Maurice, Sylvester said, "What in all of creation is this thing"

The creature was now grabbing the pickets of the fence and trying to shake it. The fence did not move at all! Adsideo could see that there was blood trickling down the pickets below each of the creature's hands.

Now that he was as close to the creature as he now was, Adsideo could see that it was hair that covered this creature. He also thought he saw a tail on this thing!

The creature then jumped up and used its feet to latch its self on to the fence.

It had strange finger shaped toes on its feet. The toes were long and it had the heels of a human foot but the rest of the foot appeared to be shaped like the palm of a hand. This made the creature appear to have two sets of arms rather than any legs. The scene was very disturbing and one that Adsideo would always remember.

"Watch out! Do not get any closer" Maurice said to Democritus "this thing could try to climb over the fence."

Arminius was standing at the rear of the group as they stood on in amazement while the animal continued with its outrage.

"This thing has a tail and fangs of a tiger," said Arminius "what kind of abomination is this"

Suddenly there was a shaking in the bushes and out jumped several more of these creatures. None of these creatures were the same; they had different markings on their bodies. Some looked like cats and some like canines of various types.

Now there were five of these animals at the fence and they were all screaming and shaking on the fence.

"It looks like we are safe from them as long as we stay on this side of the fence" said Maurice.

"Dominic, you and Colin come on over closer to us" Adsideo yelled to them "lets all stay closer together until we get out of here. Keep the Ark closer to the wall. I do not want these creatures to see it"

The creatures began to become even more erratic as Colin and Dominic came closer.

Suddenly the creatures fell to the ground as the Ark came before them. Then suddenly a small bolt of lightning burst from the Ark and struck the iron fence. The creatures then fell to their faces and began to mumble as if they were idiots in some strange babble.

As soon as the mumbling started Adsideo noticed that the other animals and birds had stopped making any noise. The forest had grown silent.

"Quickly Dominic, Colin, you two go on. Arminius, Democritus, Sylvester follow them" Adsideo said to them with out looking away from the creatures.

"The rest of us will stay behind and watch them. Hurry now we must be on our way!"

As the others rode off, Maurice and Laurence watched the animals slowly begin to raise their heads. One of them spoke.

"Who said that?" said Adsideo as he quickly as he turned his head back towards the creatures.

"One of them said something," said Maurice.

Then one of the creatures, that was closest to them stood up and began to speak some language that Adsideo had never heard before.

The creature used his hands to sign as he spoke. He seemed to be trying to tell them that they should go towards the others. The creature then began to lead them along the fence line away from Maurice, Laurence, and Adsideo. They were going the same direction as the others were headed with the Ark. Soon ahead they disappeared into the bush.

"Come on lets catch up to the others" said Maurice.

They kicked the horses and quickly sped towards the others.

"What happened?" asked Sylvester.

"They ran off in to the woods," said Adsideo "one of them tried to speak to us first and motioned that we should go this away"

"Spoke with you?" asked Dominic.

"Tried I said" replied Adsideo quickly "it spoke in some kind of language that I could not understand"

"I had never heard this language either" said Laurence "and I know quite a few languages.

They reached the southwestern corner of the room and turned to their left. They were now headed to the south and could see that there was a door casing like the one in the room of Temptation. This door was at the walls midpoint. Over the door casing was the words "Lust and Temperance"

"There is the door out of here," said Maurice let us hurry now"

Sylvester, Dominic, Colin, and Democritus were surrounding the mules and the Ark.

Maurice had taken the lead again and was followed by Adsideo. Arminius and Laurence made up the rear of the group.

Maurice was pointing to the doorway and was speaking with Adsideo.

"Look across from the doorway. There is a gate in the fence," said Maurice.

"It looks to be shut at least" replied Adsideo "I would not want those things to get loose"

"Especially if there are more of them!" said Maurice.

"Sylvester, tell the others to be aware of this gate in the fence ahead" said Adsideo.

Sylvester leaned back and told Dominic and Colin who in turn told the others behind him.

As they approached the doorway they passed within sight of the doorway past a large tree and there at the doorway was a set of the cherub statues holding the oil lamps atop of their pikes, which were held by a raised hand of the Cherubs. The ends of the lances rested at the feet of the statues.

Now, as they came closer to the statues they could also make out that the doors were the same as in the tabernacle, and at the room of Temptation.

Suddenly there was a cracking sound and a huge log which was suspended in the trees and in the fence area, came swinging downward toward the gate and hit it so hard that the steel gates came off of the hinges and spun towards the statues.

Then as quickly as this had happened out of the wooded area inside the fence came more of the creatures running out of the gate. Some of these were running and jumping. They leaped up against the trees and fences as they exited towards the doorway. There were hundreds of these creatures and about half of them stopped as they looked towards the group of Templar guards. Then they continued to run towards the Templars once again.

"Drop back towards the Ark and keep a close guard over it" said Adsideo.

"We cannot defend ourselves against so many" said Arminius "we will be over thrown"

"Do not allow the Ark to fall into these creatures hands. That was the order from God and now the order to you. Go!" said Adsideo.

As Sylvester looked back he saw a couple of the animals thrown into the air! He turned his horse around and stopped him.

"Adsideo!" yelled Sylvester "turn back this away and look"

The cherub statues had come to life and were smashing the creatures with there stone bodies. The creatures were attacking the cherubs by jumping on them and scratching and clawing at their stone bodies.

The statues were now being almost completely covered by the creatures as the scratched, clawed, and climbed on them.

The Cherubs continued to smash the creatures as if they were unnoticeable. One of the statues looked up towards the group and spoke "Hurry Templar Guards! Hurry towards the door. You must exit thought this door before the beasts resume their attack" It said to them. "The others will attack soon and we cannot keep them from breaking away and getting to you then" it said to them. "Leave the room of lust and temperance. The room of the breast!" the statue then turned and began to sling the beasts across the room. The statues continued to smash the remaining creatures as they threw some of them over the fence and back into the wooded area.

"Back to the doorway, now!" said Adsideo to the others.

They all turned and rode as fast as the horses and mules could go! They then pulled their weapons as they approached the first of the two towering statues and rode right between its legs. The Cherub swung its lance and knocked down a couple of the creatures as they ran towards the guards sending them flying backwards and over the fence.

The Cherubs both began to walk towards the gate and were smashing the creatures as they went.

Maurice and Adsideo reached the doors first and began to dismount from their horses when the doors flew open. This was due to one of the creatures being flung into the door by the Cherubs.

Maurice rode through the doorway first and was followed by Adsideo, Sylvester, and Democritus. As Maurice entered into the corridor he stuck down the creature that had stood up and could only but rise is arm towards his face before Maurice took off the hand and head of the creature. It fell to the floor in a great pile of flesh and suddenly turned into the remains of a human man.

"What kind of illusion is this?" said Arminius.

This is not illusion," replied Dominic "believe me that looked real"

"If the stroke of my blade was any indication then it was real," said Maurice "It felt real as the blade sliced the bone"

"Stop second guessing!" said Adsideo "look out there at the Cherubs." The Cherubs had continually been fighting the creatures that were still charging the statues.

Suddenly a great round but flat stone which had been hanging on the wall above the doorway fell to the ground and covered the entire surface of what had been the door opening. This spooked their horses, which took off running down the corridor. It was a hundred cubits or more before Maurice was able to get his horse stopped. He turned his horse into the center of the corridor so he would help the others stop their horses.

"Whoa" Adsideo said to his horse as he pulled it up next to Maurice "I am glad all of us were on this side of the doorway before that happen" he said to Maurice.

"Like Dominic always said, there is always something worth praise" said Colin.

"Is everyone alright?" said Adsideo.

They all reported to be in good shape but acknowledged to have been shaken. That would be with the exception of Arminius who was still reclusive.

This corridor was not like the other two that they had traveled through.

This one was built of granite block walls and cobble stone floors. It was very grand in width and had three rows of columns down the center. It was lighted by a valance of oil burning lamps that ran in a trough of fire that lead down both sides of the grand hall. There was a fountain in the middle of the four closest columns to the group. Another could be seen ahead of them.

"Let us stop and catch our breath and have a drink for the horses," said Sylvester.

"Yes and get some rest for a moment" said Adsideo "this would also be a good time to speak with Democritus about the map."

They all dismounted and each took his horse to the fountain to water them. Adsideo looked around the fountain area as he thought of the creatures that were in the room and the fence that bound them.

"Let us all rest and sleep for a couple of hours" said Dominic.

"I agree," said Adsideo "Sylvester, you and I will take the first watch and then we shall switch out"

They all agreed and began to unpack their bedrolls. Sylvester began to look for a place to make a fire but found no wood or anything to burn. He began to walk around the nearest column when he smelt bread being baked. He followed the smell to the left side of the hall. There on the other side of the last column he saw a small clay oven in the side of the wall. It had a fire burning in it but there was not any smoke coming from the fire. He opened the cover to the oven and saw the flames dancing below the clay shelf inside.

He saw that there was indeed bread that looked to be nice and brown on top. He then began to remove the bread when he suddenly heard the voice of a woman.

"Sylvester, do you remember me!" said the voice.

Sylvester turned around the room and could not see anyone there. There was something familiar about the voice. He thought of who it could be but could not remember the voice.

"Sylvester, you do disappoint me." Said the voice "you said that you loved me! Now you do not remember me," said the voice in a cynical tone.

"Who are you? Where are you?" said Sylvester "I do not know you"

Adsideo had looked around the fountain area and then took the horses from the fountain and tied them to the farthest column on the right side of the hall. The mules he had watered and then gave feed to all of the animals.

He then began to wonder about Sylvester. He did not want to disrupt the others so soon so he walked towards the other side of the hallway. He reached the left center columns when he smelt the bread and heard Sylvester's voice.

"Sylvester!" said Adsideo aloud "Sylvester where are you"

Adsideo continued to walk towards the wall and came around the corner to see Sylvester slowly turning in a circle and speaking to himself.

"Sylvester!" Adsideo yelled at the fellow Guard. "What has become of you!"?

Adsideo was now approaching Sylvester when he felt a sudden blast of cold air push him in the chest. He flew backwards off his feet and hit his head on the stone column. Adsideo was knocked out and lay there unconscious.

When Adsideo awoke Laurence was sitting over him. His head was throbbing and his vision was fuzzy.

"What happened? Where is Sylvester?" asked Adsideo.

"Sylvester found you over by the column. What hit you? Was it one of those beasts?" Laurence asked.

"The last thing I remember is looking for Sylvester and finding him dancing in a circle and babbling like an idiot!" said Adsideo.

"You must have really have hit your head hard little brother" Sylvester Quickly "I found you over by the bread oven. You were unconscious"

"No it was I who found you!" said Adsideo as he began to sit up but the pain was too much. He fell back onto the bedroll that they had put below his shoulders.

"You should rest some more before we leave" Maurice said to Adsideo.

"How long have I been out?" Adsideo asked.

"It was quite a while," answered Laurence "rest for now"

Adsideo began to mumble about how he had been pushed by something and then hit his head right as he had seen Sylvester. Adsideo sunk back to sleep.

Adsideo slept and dreamed he was back in Jerusalem guarding the doors to the. Tabernacle.

Chapter Nine

Adsideo awoke to find that he was in a travois that was pulled by his horse. The others had loaded him into this and had resumed the journey. They were still in the grand hall when he awoke and they were coming to a stop. He could not tell how far if at all they had traveled since they left the fountain area. The walls, columns, and ceiling looked the same now as they had before he had fallen unconscious.

He could hear the others talking about something that was troubling them. It seemed that they were at another set of doors and they were discussing as to which one of them was going to stay with Adsideo while the others went into the next room.

Adsideo sat up in the travois and shook his head.

"No one will need to stay with me for I am going into this room with the rest of you!" he said as he climbed out of makeshift sled.

"How far have we traveled since I hit my head?" asked Adsideo.

"We are a day and a half since we had to leave" said Maurice "you have been a sleep for two days solid"

"I will wait with him while the rest of you go inside" said Dominic.

"I am not staying out here! I am going in with the rest of you," said Adsideo angrily.

"Wait a moment, you need rest. You cannot be ready for what could be inside there," said Sylvester.

"You must think of the Guard as a whole," said Laurence "we must stay together"

"Then we will wait outside these doors until Adsideo is ready" said Sylvester.

"Are you ready of some water and food?" Democritus asked Adsideo.

"Yes I am famished," Adsideo answered.

Arminius unpacked some bread and dried meat and began to cut some of this up to give to Adsideo. Maurice brought a wineskin to Adsideo and handed it to him.

They had all began to unpack the horses and mules. For the first time in a few days Adsideo saw the Ark. It seemed to sparkle and glow as it had before. Adsideo sat there and ate his bread not saying anything. He wanted to see if the others noticed this. They did not so he continued to eat his bread while looking at the Ark. He began to daydream of the doors to the Tabernacle. He saw the doors open up and inside the room was a white marble floor with a gold inlaid terrazzo octagon border around the center of the room. He then saw that in the center of this was a picture of a mighty warrior battling a huge serpent that had the upper torso of a woman.

"Adsideo!" Yelled Arminius "have you gone deaf? Do you want some cheese to eat with the bread?"

"Adsideo are you sure you do not want to let us continued to carry you?" asked Maurice.

"No, I will be alright. I was just thinking of something." Adsideo replied as he sat the bread and wine down.

"Anything we should know about" asked Colin.

"I saw the doors to the tabernacle opening and a white marble floor. In the center of the room was the picture of a warrior fighting..."

"A woman's body attached to the body of a serpent?" asked Arminius.

"Yes! How did you know this? Asked Adsideo.

"I dreamed this last night," answered Arminius "we are in for a great battle against an evil force"

"We shall see about that," added Sylvester.

"I am sure that we will find out, sooner rather than later I am afraid." Said Laurence very cenacle.

"Why such a doubtful attitude" Dominic asked Laurence.

"I do not doubt anything of the such. I am sure we are in for the battle of our lives" Laurence replied.

"She shall engage us in total fury" said Sylvester "no one lives that opposes her!"

"What are you speaking of?" said Democritus.

"She shall endure!" shouted Laurence as he began to run towards the horses.

"I am behind you, brother!" shouted Sylvester as he came behind the heels of Laurence.

They both mounted the their horses and rode towards the doors.

"What is happening to them?" said Dominic.

Adsideo rose to his feet, dropping the bread to the ground. He then threw the wineskin over his shoulder and stood next to Maurice.

"The doors are opening for them," shouted Colin.

The two entered into the doorway and headed out of sight as the doors began to close behind them.

"Lets go after them before they become lost from our sight" said Arminius.

"What a moment" said Adsideo "lets us think about what just happened here"

"What is there to think about? Two of the Guards have abandoned their duty," said Democritus.

"Wait! Hear me out!" said Adsideo "we shall find our brothers soon enough"

Let us sit and gather strength among us. There must be no doubt in our faith before we go in there." Adsideo continued "Dominic say some words of encouragement"

"Brothers of the guard, come together as we shall triumph against the advisories of God. We have been directed by God, protected by God, and chosen by God! We shall not go without rewards for deeds completed successfully. We are not the weak ones here; we are the strong and faithful ones! We are the chosen ones! We are the triumphant ones!

As we go together before one another, ahead of and not behind, God almighty protect us. We are your servants in this world of good and evil. We shall ask for your wisdom to protect us from treachery and blasphemy." Said Dominic in a grand speech that was very much needed to sustain control of the feelings in the Guard. He continued to speak to them as all of the others gathered closer to Dominic as he spoke.

"We are the delivered and protectors of the Ark! It shall not fall into the wrong hands! We shall not fall today or any other for we are the strongest of all"

"Let us load the Ark and roll up the camp now" said Adsideo we shall find our fate behind those doors"

"You heard the Captain," said Arminius "let us find our brothers and bring them back into the fold to serve their punishments"

"There will be a trial for their crime," said Democritus "it is their right and our duty as a Templars"

"Or course you are right" said Colin "we must adhere to the code"

Colin, Arminius, Maurice, and Democritus loaded the Ark onto the mules and began to tie them to their horses.

"Maurice you and Democritus ride at the front" said Adsideo "Dominic and I will take up the rear behind the Ark"

This left Arminius and Colin riding beside the mules. They completed rolling up the rest of the bedding and utensils. After they were mounted and ready to ride. There was heard the creaking of the doors as they began to open again.

"Seems we are expected" said Dominic to Adsideo.

"We were always expected!" said Adsideo.

"Of course, as you say" said Dominic in reply.

"Lets meet this fate and show it some faith" said Arminius "for in life as in death, it is expected"

Maurice started out the lead as they began their journey once again. They headed towards the door and neither man nor beasts lowered they heads as they rode on.

They reached the doors and then stopped to look into the room before entering.

Inside they could see that there was a great fountain in the center of the room. It had carved statues of what appeared to be two wrestlers engaged in a battle of strengths. A great saucer that was suspended above the wrestlers heads, which held the great sun on one side and the moon on the other. A pair of warriors in chariots represented both the sun and the moon. As the chariots slowly moved around the saucer they caused a stream of water to fall over the edge. As if they were traveling at a faster speed and the water was cast out below the wheels of the chariots.

There was a huge set of four columns that supported the saucer above the wrestlers and was surrounded by a set of beams that went from column capital to column capital. On these beams were the hieroglyphics that had appeared to Adsideo in the room of Temptation.

There were dolphins at the four centers of the fountains base and they in turn shot a stream of water on to the wrestlers.

Surrounding the fountain, the walls of the room were covered in stone mantles, which were at different elevations and on each stood a Cherub. Each Cherub was in a different dress and held various types of weapons ranging from swords, hammers, and axes. There were two Cherubs posed as if they were flying with a net between them. In one hand they carried the net and in the other hand each carried a triad. They were also in different poses and manners of style according to era. They were in such fine detail that even their expressions were unique.

There were huge planter boxes above and below the cherubs that were filled with the largest and reddest roses that any of them had ever seen before now. They could smell the sent of the rose as they rode though the doors. There were red silk scarves draped from the planters that fell towards the floor.

They entered the central part of the room and stopped just short of the fountain. Maurice turned his horse to face the others, as did Democritus.

"I do not see anything threatening here," said Arminius "there does not appear to be a set of doors any where to be seen"

"There has to be a door out some where. Maybe this is the end of the journey," said Dominic.

"Sylvester and Laurence came in here and now they are gone. So there has to be a way out." Adsideo said.

They began to ride side-by-side around the fountain with the Ark in the center of their group as instructed by Adsideo and reiterated by Maurice. They continued on around the radius of the fountain and reached the backside of the fountain. Against the far wall there was an eight to ten seat box with a throne and adjoining seats next to it. There was a marble railing and balusters that divided the throne from the room's floor. Tapestries covered the wall and were hung behind the seats.

It was as if this was an arena or throne room for some unknown King.

"This could be some kind of a trap," warned Maurice. "This appears to be a room for judgments to be made"

"I think it is a trap of some kind," repeated Maurice.

"Calm down everyone" said Adsideo "let us not jump to conclusions"

"Over there is where Laurence and Sylvester could have gone," Colin said as he pointed toward the Tapestries.

On the other side of the room they could hear the doors, which they had entered through beginning to shut.

"I knew it was a trap," said Maurice again.

Suddenly from behind the curtain several young women appeared. They were dressed in short silk tunics of different colors and trimmings. One of the last to enter prepared the thrones that sat in the center of the box.

Then out from behind the tapestry came a pair of women that were identical in every way conceivable to the eye.

They were dressed in the same clothes and wore the same hairstyle of wavy black hair pulled into a ponytail. Nestled on top of their heads were thin golden crowns with inlays of pearls and various colored gems. Right in the center of each crown was a tiger-eye stone.

The twins entered the box seat area and walked down the first short set of steps and turned onto the isle where the thrones were at, then sat next to each other in the throne seats in unison. Then one of the women dressed in a blue tonic stepped forward and approached the railing where she came to a stop. She rested her right arm on the railing and began to speak.

"You may present yourselves now!" said the woman "you shall start with the leader first"

"We are all Templar Guards and this is all you will get from us. Until we are released from this room and we know whom it is we are addressing" said Adsideo.

"So you are the leader," said the woman in blue.

"I am the leader," said Arminius.

"No, I am the leader," said Dominic.

"You are always trying to claim leadership," said Democritus to Dominic "I am truly the leader" said Democritus as he turned back to face the woman in blue.

"I am the leader" shouted Maurice as he looked at the woman and then back to the group.

They all began to appear to argue with each other as if to confuse the women as they watched on.

"Cease this fodder" said the woman very loudly "you shall obey us as your new masters or you shall be punished"

"We shall have to see who bows to who" shouted Colin "as he began to ride towards the front of the others. All of a sudden Colin felt his muscle and flesh begin to harden and felt as if it would crack. He came to a stop almost as soon as he could feel the tightening of his body. His lungs, heart and other organs seemed to function but he could not move even his chest to breathe.

The others saw Colin's body turn to a white polished marble. His horse and all of his gear on it turned to this marble as well. This made them look like a statue to honor some local hero in some small town square.

"What have you done to our brother?" said Arminius as he began to ride towards the figure of Colin.

"Stop where you are at" said Adsideo quickly do not move any further. We need all of us together"

"What kind of witchery is this that you possess" asked Dominic "I have studied magic of all kinds and have never heard of this ability"

"Shall we demonstrate this again for you to be convinced?" said the woman in blue.

"You shall find that we Templars also have a magic power," said Dominic "we call it the faith and will of God"

"Stop the talking and start explaining who you are and how we might leave this place," said Arminius.

"We wish only peace from you" said Adsideo "but we have a mission to complete and we are in a hurry"

"Sorry you disgusting men but, no one has ever left here!" said the woman "you shall learn obedience to the Fates" the other women began to laugh and giggle.

"What is there that seems to be so amusing about this," asked Democritus.

"Silence" said one of the twins as she stood and began to walk towards the railing "you shall not speak at anytime unless asked to"

The other twin stood and approached the railing and stood at her sister's right-hand side.

The second twin began to wave her left hand and spoke a language that none of the Templars had ever heard. They heard Colin begin to breath as he let out a gasp of air. Then Colin began to resume his natural self again. His horse, like Colin, had resumed its natural body movement once again.

"Stop your trickery," said Adsideo "we do not wish you any harm. We are to be on our way."

"You shall not speak again," roared the first twin then suddenly a leather mask covered his face and bound Adsideo' s mouth.

"Stop this…" as Dominic tried to speak suddenly all of the Templars were gagged by the same masks as Adsideo wore. Then out of the sidewalls of the courtyard thin doors opened and a mass of women dressed in breastplates and armed with lances and swords surrounded the Templar guard.

"That shall keep you obedient" said the twins in unison. Again the women began to giggle. Beyond the hearing of the Templars and hidden by the giggling laughter of the other women the twins whispered to each other.

"These males will work as fine mates," said the first twin to the second twin.

"They will do just fine, I will give no contest your distribution of these men" the second replied to her sister.

"Bring the men about for us to see," said the first twin to the women "we shall have a feast tonight in honor of our new catch"

"Sister, you should not forget to thank father Bellabezzer for bringing them to us" said the second twin as her mouth formed a small and slender grin.

"Yes he will be very pleased when we deliver this Ark of the Covenant to him. He will bury us in admiration" said the first twin to the second.

Now these twins were daughters of the evil one which had thwarted Colin and Arminius in the room of Temptation. Their father cast them into this room after they witnessed the accidental murder of their mother by his own hand. They were kept here in a section of the caverns that was not escapable by anyone.

Their father and all others who knew of them knew them as the witches of the Fates.

As the Templar Guards were brought in front of the twins they were lined up in a row with the first of the Guards, who happened to be Arminius, facing the twins and the other guards were filed behind Arminius.

"You will be allowed to speak your names and then you shall remain silent. Any disruptions and the punishment will be much more severe then before" said the first of the twins whose name was Daphne.

Once again the second twin, whose name was Desiree, began to wave her arms and speak in the odd language, the gags disappeared from the Templars mouths as if they had never been there at all.

"What is your name" Daphne asked the first of the guards before her.

"Arminius is my name" he responded.

"You shall pick from any of the women before you to become your host" Daphne told him "the only thing is that you must pick now"

"I do not see any that are befitting my kind," replied Arminius.

Now the other guards remained silent as this conversation continued.

"You look like a human to me. What do you mean your kind?" asked Daphne.

"My kind must be clean and pure before I can take them as mate" replied Arminius "It would be a mockery of all I have been taught and would rather die than lay with such filth"

"Then it shall be!" said Daphne as she raised her arms in anger and began to speak in the foreign language. Then Desiree nudged her sister and said, "Do not hurt him for we need all eight of them"

Then Daphne lowered her arms and began to stare at Arminius with such a glare that he thought he might burst into flames or something else as painful. She then slightly smiled as she began to speak to him in a much deeper tone of voice. He thought he saw her eyes become a glowing green color for a moment.

"These women are all virgins and are of the purest forms. You shall pick one now!" yelled Daphne.

This caused all of the room to shake and sent the horses and the two mules scurrying about the room. The Cherub statues could be seen and heard as they teetered on their ledges.

"Alright! All right! I will pick one of these "fair" women as you wish," said Arminius quickly.

He began to walk towards the twins when his legs began to lock up and his feet stopped in their tracks.

"What are you doing, fool?" asked Daphne.

"You told me to pick and I wish to see each of them closer before I make my selection" replied Arminius "now let me go!"

Desiree leaned toward her sister and said, "He is strong willed, father will be proud once we have broken his spirit."

Arminius found a blond haired woman with the most amazing green eyes that he had even seen before.

"I shall take this one," he said.

"Her name is Emerald," said Desiree "Emerald, take Arminius to the side for a moment until the others have picked their mates"

The other guards that had been watching this scenario that had not been looking for their choice of women now began to do so.

"I shall take the one in the yellow tunic," said Colin "the dark headed one over there"

Colin walked toward his choice and as he did he turned and looked at Adsideo and winked. He then turned back towards the woman he had selected. He took her by the hand and stood next to Arminius and his selection.

"Her name is Corinth," said Desiree.

Adsideo spoke up as he had his eye on the woman in blue who had been speaking to them in the beginning. "I will take the speaker in blue" he said to the twins.

"You have made a fine selection" said Desiree "now what is your name and we will introduce you to Sapphire"

"My name is Adsideo" he replied as he began towards Sapphire. He then turned to Dominic and applied the same wink that Arminius had given to him. He then took his place next to Arminius and Colin.

Dominic having seen both Colin and then Adsideo wink had caught on to what was happening. He turned to Maurice and whispered, "tell Democritus to play along for now"

Dominic said "what is the name of the redheaded woman in the white tunic?"

"Her name is Gardenia," said Desiree "she will make a fine mate. I must warn you that She is very stubborn.

Dominic took his place with the other guards whom had chosen. Then it was Maurice's turn to pick.

"I would like to pick the two dark skinned ones," said Maurice.

"So you are the first to pick more than one" said Daphne "you may proceed with your selection and this will be encouraged. Their names are Marta and Bella"

Maurice took the selected ones at each side of him and stood next to the others.

Democritus said, "I will also pick two but they are to be selected by their own choice"

"This cannot be permitted," said Daphne "there cannot be any choice made in this manner for they will all want to select."

"Then there shall be a vote held for the ones that are to be mine," said Democritus.

"No there will not be a vote," replied Daphne "they will be appointed by me and my sister"

Federla and Republia shall be your mates by my order," said Daphne.

Federla was very tall for a woman and had dirty blond colored hair. She was very attractive and had been well trained in the art of warfare. Republia was of medium build and weight and had the darkest black hair that Democritus had ever seen. She was very beautiful and very sensuous. Democritus could not have selected this well on his own with as many choices and was glad to have had the twins select them for him.

"Now all of you shall be taken to the festival of the fertility that will be held in your honor. This will be the first of its kind in over fifteen years" said Daphne "may the thoughts and gifts of our father be upon you as you dance and feast."

"We must be allowed to take the Ark with us at all times" said Dominic.

"It will be taken care of" replied Desiree "trust us, nothing will happen to it"

"Nothing can happen to it!" said Adsideo "he looked at the others and motioned with a nod of his head for them to comply with Desiree.

They were led through one of the side-hidden doors out of the great fountain room and into a tunnel. This tunnel led to another large columned room. There were six columns, which were in a double row; side-by-side and sitting atop a raised center area. There was a set of steps that was four steps high. All of this was made of pink colored granite. In the center of the column rows was a setting of food sitting on top of a large wooden table.

The smell of roasted meat and steamed squash was filling the air. There were other fruits and vegetables on the table and many that they were not familiar with. There were chairs on each side of the table and each was carved from head to toe with the glyphs that were seen in the room of Temptation. Around each leg was a carving of a snake's body wrapping its self around and around until finally reaching the top of the chair back. Its head was resting on the top and seemed to be positioned to look over the occupants shoulder.

At the far end of the table sat Laurence and Sylvester with two other women.

"Look over their, our two lost sheep" Arminius said to Adsideo and the others as he walked along behind them.

"Yes, I see them" Adsideo replied to him. "We shall soon learn what they know of this place."

"Please sit wherever you would like to and we will serve you" Gardenia said to them.

"Please, sit," added Republia.

The Templar Guards all began to sit at the table for the smell of the food was very strong and seemed to weaken their legs. This made them willing participants for the feast.

Maurice leaned over to where Adsideo and Arminius were beginning to sit down and whispered to them.

"Let us call Laurence and Sylvester down here and see what they have been doing since running away"

"I agree," said Arminius as he and Adsideo nodded in agreement.

Maurice stood up and yelled down at the other end of the table to Laurence "Laurence come and see your brothers"

Laurence never even looked up, for his focus was in the conversation with a blond headed woman.

"Laurence do not ignore your brothers"

Chapter Ten

"Take the Ark from the beasts and prepare the alter room for the prayers to for our father!" shouted Desiree to the other remaining women. The women servants began to catch the horses that had been frightened earlier. The mules were wandering around the fountain and were easily caught. The first two women to catch the mules began to remove the blue and gold covering for the Ark when out of no where came a strong blast of wind so quick that it blew the top of the Ark high into the air almost hitting the ceiling. Then came a very powerful suction of all the air that was in the room. Consuming the women guards but not the twins and the furnishings of the room. Each of the consumed women had disappeared into sand as the Ark swallowed them. The lid came crashing down onto the Ark as it now was sparkling and glowing with the green colored haze. Then the Ark disappeared from sight. The twins also disappeared from sight in their own way, through the doorway behind the tapestry. This led to a tunnel, which led to a hallway. At the end of the hallway was a balcony which over looked the alter room. As they reached this balcony they turned and ran to their left and down to the end of the hallway. Then they turned and ran down the stairs that led to the alter room. This alter was dedicated to their father and had him in effigy all over the room. A great stone image of him stood behind the Alter, and it was facing at the doorway in which they entered. Both of them dropped to their knees and began to weep. They were mumbling in the strange tongue which they had used to cast the spells on the Templars once before.

What happened next was a surprise to even them. An image of their father appeared above the alter. It was a transparent image that seemed as if it was alive with his soul. This image was in fact the very transformation of their father's black soul.

Their father said to them in a scow "where is the only thing that I have asked of you in return for all I have given you? I shall take pence on you for your unworthiness to be my offspring! I shall see to it that you will destroy these "Templars" you shall destroy them now!"

In that time the two twins were turned in to smoky sand that fell into a pile on the stone alter room floor. But then out of the sand came another rising wisp of smoke that grew and grew. It began to rise into a larger and thicker smoke that was turning from a bluish green to a red colored smoke. Then a transformation of a different kind began, for out of the smoke grew two very large creatures. Yet still alive! They had very large heads for their size and hair that was so oily that it clung to their bony necks. Their backs were humped as if they were very old women and their arms remained pulled up towards their torsos. They whined and sneered as they tried to form their first words with their new mouths. It sounded excruciating as they bellowed out words very clumsy and awkward.

"What can we do for our father but fall to our knees as he changes us into these pathetic forms." Sneered Daphne "shall we eat our weight in Templars to please you"

"Oh, you are as hungry as I am I see!" said Desiree.

"Shut up! You ugly excuse for a being" said Bellabezzer "I have given you this punishment for losing the Ark. You will be like this forever more unless you correct this situation. I have taken your hearts from your bodies and you shall be as heartless as you have proven to be foolish!

Now take the passage to the dining room and kill them! Eat of his or her flesh for every one you eat your beauty shall return little by little. Find the Ark and return it here to me and I will forgive you. Until then get out of my sight!" the image of Bellabezzer disappeared and the room fell silent.

"Yes, sister let us be on our way," said Desiree as she let out a cackling laugh that echoed throughout the chamber.

The Guards all sat down with the exception of Maurice who called to Laurence and Sylvester at the other end of the long table.

"Laurence if you will not speak to your brothers then they will speak to you" said Maurice as he walked to the other end of the table.

Marta and Bella began to make a place at the table for him as he kept speaking to Laurence and then Sylvester.

As he approached the two wayward brothers, they continued not to acknowledge Maurice's presence or even his existence.

The others had begun to grab at the fruits and the drinks that were on the table. They were speaking among each other, and watching Maurice at the other end of the table.

Adsideo continued to watch Maurice and something did not feel right. Something was wrong here.

He looked back down to where Maurice was at and saw that he was finally down to the opposite end of the table.

Maurice walked on the left side of the table and walked passed Sylvester.

Maurice turned and stood at the very end of the table and slammed his fist down very quickly. He glanced down to the other end of the table towards the other Templars and then back to Sylvester and Laurence.

"Why do you chose to play this farce with us" said Maurice.

The two looked up at him as though they did not recognize him. Then Laurence turned back to the woman at the opposite side of the table from him and began to speak with her again.

"Laurence, do not turn away from me. I wish to speak with you," shouted Maurice "I said do not turn away from me!" repeated Maurice as he struck Laurence. Laurence tumbled off of the seat and landed on his back. He hit the stone floor quickly and his head snapped backwards and hit the floor. He was knocked un-conscience.

Sylvester who had stopped speaking to his companion as soon as Maurice had struck Laurence watched until Laurence was knocked out and then turned back to the woman and began to speak to her. As if nothing had happened.

"What is wrong with you?" said Maurice as he swung his arms back to his right and knocked all of the food and wine over on top of Sylvester.

Sylvester stood up and brushed the food from his chest plate and then from his kilt.

That was when Maurice realized it was the women that were somehow enchanting them.

Maurice drew his sword and ran it through the blond that was sitting next to Sylvester and there was a screeching sound as she disappeared into a wisp of smoke. He saw this and then turned to the dark headed woman that had sat down on the ground next to Laurence, she had his head in her hands as Maurice lopped off her head. She also let out a scream as she turned into the same colored wisp of smoke.

Maurice looked down to the opposite end of the table and saw Adsideo rise up and draw his sword. Adsideo had been the only one of the other Templars that witnessed what had happened at Maurice's end of the table.

"Adsideo, wait for me to help you!" shouted Maurice as he ran towards the other end of the table.

Adsideo raised his sword and began slicing with it.

Adsideo was into his second victim as Maurice reached him to assist and they both completed the killings of the women.

"Hey, where are we?" asked Dominic.

"What is going on here?" asked Democritus as he looked at the floor and then back up to the others.

There was a state of confusion among them.

Adsideo and Maurice began to speak to them as to console them and explain what had just happened.

Maurice then ran down to the other end of the table to check on Sylvester and Laurence. He found that Sylvester had awoken Laurence who was still lying on the ground. They were confused as to where they were and what had happened to them.

Maurice then began explaining what had happened to them. He had them stand up and began to lead them back to the other end of the table to regroup with the others.

"Maurice how are they" asked Adsideo.

"They will be fine. Laurence has a bump on his head but he will be alright," replied Maurice.

"Let us get back to the judgment room and find the Ark," said Adsideo to the rest of the others.

"Remember brothers we were bewitched and enchanted by the witches. There is no fault of our own so keep your heads up and look for the Ark," said Adsideo.

"We shall find it. Do not worry. Remember that we are volatile while it is gone and we shall have to watch ourselves very carefully" said Maurice.

"Let us be on our way!" said Adsideo.

The Templar Guards ran through the corridor, which led from the dining room to the Judgment room with the fountain of the wrestlers.

As they entered the area they could tell that most of the lights had been extinguished and it was very dark in the room. The light that was left lit, shimmered and reflected off of the water in the fountain. Both off the top saucer and off the pool at the base. This caused the reflection to send faint streams of light off into various directions. There were dead roses where there had been live ones earlier.

"This is not the same room is it?" asked Democritus.

"Yes it is, just different," said Arminius "let us ride to the other side of this fountain and see if we can open the door"

"No, follow me to the box seat area and let us see what is behind the tapestry that the twin's came out of" said Maurice.

They decided that Maurice, Adsideo, Laurence, and Arminius would go in search of the Ark and the others would stay in this room and try to find the horses and then break though the door to the outside.

"Be careful and may God be with you," said Dominic as the others jumped over the railing.

Colin and Sylvester paired together and walked around the left side of the fountain and Dominic and Democritus walked around the right side. They were in search of the animals.

Both pairs of the men met around the other side of the fountain and then began to walk with each other once more.

"Look, there is a couple of the horses over in the shadows," said Democritus "I will go and get them. Dominic you and the others wait on me here"

"Hold on a moment," said Dominic "let us all go together"

Sylvester and Colin agreed and they walked one abreast to the other. As they approached the corner where the horses were seen they could see that there was only the two of them at this location. There was no sign of the mules though. They fanned out and cornered the horses that were still a bit spooked.

Colin and Democritus gathered their reins. These two horses had been Maurice and Arminius' s and still had their gear on them.

"Alright let us look over towards the door for the rest of them," said Dominic "that is the only place left that they could be at"

"Unless they took them into one of the hidden side doors of the seating area," said Colin.

"Let us go to the entry doors first then we will speculate from there," said Dominic.

"Dominic you and Sylvester take the two horses and ride while we walk." Said Colin.

"Age before beauty" said Dominic.

The horses were thirsty and hungry and seemed to be weak and unwilling.

Dominic and Sylvester mounted the horses and then they headed to the entry doors. The came up to the doors rather quickly and discovered that the doors were open. Sylvester began to ride though the doorway when Dominic yelled to him.

"Do not ride though the doorway!" shouted Dominic "wait on Colin and Democritus to catch up to us"

Adsideo and the others entered into the doorway hidden by the tapestry and found the corridor leading to the balcony area. As they reached the balcony they stopped and looked over the railing down onto the alter room.

"Look at that down there" said Laurence.

"Whose image is that?" said Maurice.

"It is the evil one I told you of from the room of Temptation. He is the one who tried to reach out and get us. He is known as Bellabezzer the dark destroyer," said Arminius "his evil army is locked in the northern wall of the room of Temptation and is repressed there by all of the good things left on the earth.

It is said that on the day that the last good deed is done for your fellow man, then the evil one and his army will be allowed to ride out into the world. That is when mankind will see it's last sunset forever"

"This looks like a place of worship to him," said Maurice.

"Who would want to worship evil?" said Laurence.

"There are many that we have all seen before that do not know good in their own hearts," said Adsideo.

"Maurice, you have seen this before"

"Yes, you are right. I guess I never thought of them as being Godless. I never thought of them as worshipping such evil things." said Maurice.

"Well now you know and when we get back to the others and have time I am sure that Dominic would be glad to teach you more on the worship of other ethnic groups" said Laurence "I know of some very strange customs that I have learned though out my travels for King Solomon"

"Alright, before history class begins let us concentrate on our goals at hand," said Arminius "I have seen this entity at work and I do not like what I remember of him"

"I hope he is still entrapped in the wall in the room of Temptation" Arminius continued "you do not want this one loose on the face of the earth"

"I am afraid it is not that simple," said Adsideo "there will always be evil where there is good. One will not work without the other"

"It is all about the checks and balances that God wishes men to abide by," said Laurence "we must respect both but strive to appease our Lord by doing the right thing in his eyes"

"Let us find the Ark and get out of here as soon as possible" said Maurice.

They continued down the hall until they reached the end of it. This is where the stairs leading down to the alter were located. They began down the stairs and soon found themselves at the alter room floor and standing in front of the alter. Then once again appeared the image of Bellabezzer. He was in full figure but in a ghostly state of existence. He was only standing there in spirit alone and did not seem a threat other then what may come out of his foul mouth.

"How dare you enter this place? You are not worthy of this room. You are not worthy of standing before me much less in my sanctuary," said the evil apparition "you are weak and disgusting to me"

"Well from here the stench of your breath alone is enough to make my eyes water, you abomination of man," said Maurice.

"Allow me to handle this," said Adsideo "when you speak to a soldier of God's holy temple, you had better tremble with respect. For he could one day become your Master."?

"God? I will teach you a few things about God," said Bellabezzer "the reason I am where I am now, in a wall of a room with my army. Imprisoned by God due to my strength and power over weak men" the evil one continued "we are kept in such a place because we are the most powerful in the universe and would have conquered all life, had God not been so afraid of me and my power"

"Well if this twisted bit of information is what you offer as reasoning then no wonder your followers are as stupid as the ones that we have encountered so far" said Adsideo "who do you think created you? And if you are so powerful then release your army and be free. Oh, I forgot you lack the intelligence of the enlightenment of good, or in your case just plain common sense"

"I shall show you some common sense little man" said Bellabezzer. He raised his arms as the anguish began to show in his expression. His face changed to a deep shade of anger. His armor with the anguishing souls began to scream as before. He thrust his arms down and forward and from the palms of his hands came a green fireball that burst forth and barely missed the Templar guards as each jumped for cover.

Adsideo rolled over and away from the alter, and then back onto his feet. Maurice had jumped to his right and then behind one of the stone figures that lined the center of the room.

As Maurice turned and looked he could see that Laurence was behind a stone figure that was next in line to his.

Arminius was behind Adsideo and had dropped down to the ground.

"come on, Arminius" said Adsideo "let us get to the alter and face the fear. He will not destroy men of faith"

They both lunged forward and jumped onto the alter. The image of Bellabezzer began to falter and flicker as though it would disappear, but it did not. Once again Bellabezzer raised his arms and this time he began to speak the strange language and lowered his arms down to deliver another blow. As he did this Maurice and Laurence ran and jumped onto the alter to join Adsideo in whatever it was he was planning to do. They now were surrounding the figure of Bellabezzer and each slowly was turning around him in a circle as if he would try and run from them.

Then came the blast of green fire from each of Bellabezzer palms that sent all of them flying backwards and each hitting the floor with a thud. This could be heard very clearly to each since they seemed to hit the floor at the same time.

Again they each jumped up without thinking and ran towards the image without fear. Adsideo lunged forward with his arms out reached in front of him and each of his hands opened in a crescent as if to grab the evil one by his throat. As he almost had him by the throat the image disappeared into nothingness.

As Adsideo landed on his knees and slid across the alter knocking Arminius off of his feet he screamed,

"Where have you gone too. Are you a coward?"

"Do not call him back on my account" said Arminius as he stood up from the alter room floor where he had landed after Adsideo had knocked him down.

"I agree," said Laurence that was close. Let him go away from here for now."

"We should face him here and now!" said Maurice "this is not a foe I want to ponder on meeting again"

"Let us stay on this side of the door," said Dominic "I have a feeling that if we go through the door opening then they will close on us again and we will be cut off from the others."

"You could be right of course," replied Sylvester.

Sylvester turned Adsideo' s horse back toward the direction that they had just come from to see if he could see Colin and Democritus. He could not but kept watching for them. After a moment more he could see their smoky shapes begin to appear from the dusky glow of the room behind them.

"Let us ride back and pick them up and come back here," said Sylvester.

They rode up and picked up Colin and Democritus. Once they were on the backs of the horses they turned the horses back towards the doorway and before they reached the door they saw that the doors were now closed.

"What did I tell you?" said Dominic "I knew that if we went though we would still be on the other side of them now.

"Yes, yes, you are right old one" said Sylvester "while you baste in your own flavor let the rest of us determine where the horses and mules have gone"

There from behind them was the whinny of one of the horses. They turned and looked back at the direction of the sound and saw the other six horses and the two mules come into the murky light at the edge of the fountain area. Then suddenly there were two disgusting figures of women that had herded them with whips and who kept lashing the whips in the air and popping them at the heels of the horses.

"Come and get what is left of your precious cargo," Daphne cackled.

Democritus looked at the others and then back to the twin witches and shouted, "let us retrieve the Ark from these hideous creatures"

"Let us go," shouted Dominic as he pulled back on the reins of the horse and then released them as he kicked the horse into a Gallup. Sylvester did the same as they pushed the horses into full runs.

The two sisters saw the Templars coming and began to prepare for their attack. They both threw down their whips and began to raise their arms and speak in the strange magical language. They began to chant the same foreign words together. As the Templars approached they saw these two evil twins turn into a pair of giant cobras with the wretched faces of the witches. They had fangs of the great snakes protruding from their mouths and these seemed to secrete golden colored venom that ran down their chins. They had greasy looking hair on top of their heads and this swung wildly as each of the sisters began to strike at the Templar Guards one after the other.

"Dominic, you and Sylvester distract them while I rush in below their bodies" said Democritus "Colin come with me and try to slice their bellies"

"I am with you! Come on let us go!" said Colin as they both jumped off of the backs of the horses and began to run towards the giant snakes. As they began to run forward Desiree saw them and struck first at Colin, causing him to leap away from her and then fall to the ground. Then Democritus ran towards her and as she tried to strike Colin again he drove his sword into one of her eyes. Desiree quickly lifted her head and Democritus held onto his sword and was carried high into the air. Colin leaped to his feet and ran towards the huge snake.

Colin drew his sword and held it high over his head, as he ran towards Desiree he screamed in fury.

Democritus was flung upwards and swung over his sword and landed on top of Desiree's head standing on his feet. He held onto the hilt of his sword and rode like he was breaking a wild animal.

Democritus saw Colin running towards Desiree but lost sight of him as Desiree took a strike at Dominic's horse and rider.

As Desiree struck at Dominic, Democritus was flung to the floor. He lost his grip with his sword and it was still stuck in the head of the evil beast as he hit the floor.

Colin ran at the serpents belly and slashed it open with the first swing. Having now over run the snake he turned and jumped onto its back and began hacking.

Daphne had knocked Sylvester from his horse and was striking at him as Dominic was trying to distract her from him. Dominic waved his sword in the air and yelled at her while circling around Sylvester. Democritus ran and caught the horse that Sylvester had been riding and pulled the spare sword that all riders carried and ran to help Colin as he continued to hack at the serpent Desiree.

As Democritus approached Desiree he heard her scream in her human voice and he saw that Colin had mortally wounded her by cutting her in half. The first of the twins fell to the floor dead.

Democritus then turned and ran towards Daphne. He increased his speed as he approached her. Just as he came up to her, she snatched Dominic from the horse and whipped her head high into the air. Democritus reached the last of the twins and plunged his sword in between her black shining scales causing her to drop Dominic to the ground.

Dominic lay there motionless and seemed to be unconscious.

Daphne screaming the whole time as she swayed back and forth and finally falling to the ground. Two of the horses whinnied at the same time and bolted towards the fountain and disappeared to the other side of it.

Democritus ran over to the giant head of Desiree that now lie still on the judgment room floor and pulled his sword from the top of her head.

"Sylvester! Colin! Are you all right! Come and help me with Dominic, he is hurt" said Democritus.

"Maurice, I think we should go on and leave this place and be thankful he is gone for now" said Adsideo.

"I know I would feel a little more confident if I knew where they had put the Ark"

"Let's get busy and look in here for it and then lets go" said Laurence.

"You sound scared little brother," said Arminius.

"I have seen images of this demon before" said Laurence "In temples of the Kelts. He is said to not only to be an eater of men's souls but also there flesh and bone. There were glyphs of him consuming large quantities of men each day"

Arminius and Maurice had all ready begun to search around the effigy columns for any sign of the Ark. There was nothing to be found!

Of all the rooms they had found, one would think it would be here of all places! Thought Adsideo to himself.

"Begin to feel along the wall panels for hidden doors" said Adsideo "Laurence, you look over by the outer walls, and I will search this alter"

Adsideo walked around the alter and inspected its construction. It was approximately one cubic tall, made of a red granite, it was cobbled stone on the top and sides. It was level in its top and there were the life sized statues of

Bellabezzer around half of the alters circumference. There were six of these statues in all. They appeared to have come from different eras or cultures. There were none of them the same in design.

An evil demon worshiped by many different kinds of people, Adsideo thought to himself. Why would God allow such evil to exist? What was the purpose of having evil men? Was it living examples of what types of souls would perish at death for the rest of us to see during our own existence?

Adsideo continued to search along the outer ledge of the alter when he found the head of a Ram carved flush in the surface of the vertical sidewall of the alter, where it met the surface of the lower floor.

Adsideo stuck his index and middle finger of his right hand into the hollow eye sockets of the ram's skull and the floor of the alter began to collapse into a hidden spiral staircase.

"Maurice, Laurence, Arminius look at what I found!" yelled Adsideo "let us find out where this leads too!"

"It could be a trap," said Maurice.

"I doubt that a set of stairs would be a trap," said Laurence "it would not make sense"

"I will take a look down their first," said Arminius "the three of you stay here and I will yell up to you once I reach the bottom of the staircase"

"Alright, but you must stay in constant contact with us by yelling back" said Adsideo.

Arminius began down the stairs. He grabbed the first of the wall-hung torches that he came across and carried it with him. Holding it above his head and in front of himself, He continued down the steps and came to the bottom after spiraling down one and a half turns. He then reached a small vestibule with a door facing him.

"There is a door that swings out at the bottom of the stairs and I am at it now" Arminius yelled up to the others.

"Open the door and tell us what you see," Adsideo yelled down to him in reply.

Arminius opened the door, which did not make a sound while being opened; this told him that it must have been used quite often.

Once opened he saw that he was at the room of judgment once again and that this doorway was at the base of the fountain of the huge wrestlers.

"I am standing at the base of the wrestlers fountain in the room of judgment" Arminius yelled though the doorway and urged the others to join him. Soon they were all four standing back in the room of judgment.

"Look!" said Laurence "there is our horses"

"I do not see the mules though," said Maurice "and the Ark must be with them"

"Each of you get your horses and spread out to look for the others. Laurence you get the remaining horses secured and wait for us to return," said Adsideo.

Maurice, Arminius, and Adsideo mounted their horses and rode around the other side of the fountain. Once on the other side they could see the other Templars a short distance away from them. They were over towards the door, which had led them into this cursed room originally.

Adsideo could see that there were only three figures standing there ahead of him.

"Sylvester? Democritus? Dominic? Colin? Is that you?" yelled Adsideo.

"Who is missing from the Group?" no one answered him so he thought that it was possible that they could not hear him.

Then he turned to the others and said, "Come on Maurice, let us gather our flock and find the Ark"

As they rode up to the other three of their group, they saw the huge snakes lying dead on the floor of the room.

"Looks like you have been as busy, as we have been!" said Maurice He saw that Dominic was laying on the ground. "What happened to Dominic?" said Maurice as he dismounted the horse he was riding and began to attend to his fallen friend. Democritus was cradling Dominic's head and he was tearful as he told Maurice that he did not believe that Dominic was going to live. There was a gasp from Dominic's lips as he tried to speak. His body quivered and his hands trembled as he contorted his face to speak.

"You must take my body to the fountain, please promise me this" Dominic said and then he became unconscious. Maurice reached up with his left hand and felt of Dominic's throat and then his forehead.

"His skin is balmy. I believe he has passed," said Maurice as he looked to Democritus.

"Hurry! Help me load him onto my horse. I will take him to the fountain" said Maurice.

"Wait! We do not have enough horses for all us to ride back on," said Democritus.

"We will have to leave a couple of you here while we ride back and get some more horses" said Adsideo "we will not be long"

"Colin, Arminius, you two stay here, or begin to walk back, and we will come back with your horses," said Adsideo as they began to ride off towards the fountain.

"So what happened here?" Arminius asked Colin as the others rode off. Colin began to tell Arminius what had happened to the twin witches after making Arminius promise to tell about their adventure behind the hidden door. Arminius listened with total concentration as Colin told their tale.

"Laurence! Laurence!" yelled Maurice to Laurence as they approached the fountain "take two horses with you and ride to the entry doors! We left Colin and Arminius there because we did not have enough horses. Please go and get them"

Laurence saw the body of Dominic over Maurice's horse as Maurice dismounted from it.

"What has happened?" Laurence asked, "What is wrong with Dominic?"

"He is dead" Maurice replied "Adsideo, help me get him down and over to the fountain. It was his wish"

Laurence and Sylvester rode off towards the entry door to pick up Colin and Arminius.

Adsideo and the others, which had tied their horses, went over to help Maurice take Dominic's body down. They sat his body down onto the edge of the fountain base and removed his armor, sword, and girth.

Adsideo took a cloth from his own girth and sunk it into the fountain and cleaned Dominic's face with it.

"Democritus, what happened?" asked Adsideo.

"Help me place him in the fountain" said Maurice.

"What?" said Adsideo "why are we doing this?"

"It is what he told us to with his body" Democritus snapped back "It is what we will do!"

"Hold on a moment" said Sylvester "let us wait on the others to get here before we put him to rest"

Chapter Eleven

"Colin! Arminius! Come on we have to get back to the others!" Laurence yelled to them as he rode up to the two them. He had brought their horses and they mounted them quickly.

"Where are the others?" asked Arminius.

"They are at the fountain waiting on us," answered Laurence "come on lets go!"

They rode off as fast as they could and headed straight for the fountain. They arrived quickly. They saw that the body of Dominic had been undressed, bathed, and laid on the edge of the fountain. They rode over to the other horses and tied theirs up next to them.

"Come gather with us as we commit our brother's body to the earth," said Sylvester to Arminius and Colin "he will surely be missed"

Adsideo stood up on the fountains base and spoke above his brother's heads as he recited some of the times he could remember spending with Dominic while serving King Solomon and while on this journey with the Ark.

"I would like to say that if any man was more deserving to seek God. He will have a lot to stand up too, for he was a fine and righteous man. And I will now let his body be given to the water of this fountain which I hear was his dieing request"

They had torn one of the tapestries down and had laid his body on it. It was now draped under his body and they were prepared to allow him to slowly slip into the water when suddenly there was a change in the surroundings that made all of them stop what they were doing and look around.

The air seemed to change and there was a change in the lighting. The light seemed to come from another place other than from the room.

As the room brightened they saw that the cherub statues that lined the room on there various perches seemed to be alive as they began to fly around the room. One of the first to fly from its perch flew straight up and joined with several others way above their heads. The Templars lost sight of these cherubs as they flew into the brightest of the light at the very center of the ceiling. The fountain saucer blocked their view of this. Very quickly the cherubs reappeared and they were carrying the Ark!

"Look at what they are bringing! It is the Ark!" Said Sylvester.

The Cherubs descended slowly and sat the Ark down between the fountain and the horses. The light made the air itself seem to shimmer. Then the Ark began to glow with the green mist and it also seemed to sparkle as it had before.

"Guards of the Tabernacle, take back possession of the Ark of the Covenant," said one of the Cherubs. "We must remain here at the fountain of good verses evil. It is our duty to support Good in its never-ending battle with Evil. You must however, take the Ark from this place and take it to its resting place at the feet of God. When we saw that the twins were about to give it to their father we made it disappear and hid it from them until we could give it back to you. Maurice figured out the spells of the witches that you dined with earlier so fast that we did not have to rescue you like the ones before you. What we do not understand is why their spells did not work on you Adsideo nor on Maurice"

"Where do we go from here?" Adsideo asked the Cherub that had been speaking "we have searched this room and have looked through every door"

"Follow us and you will be shown the way" was the reply. The light remained so bright that they could not tell which one of the Cherubs was speaking. Adsideo turned both directions to see that all of the other Templars were looking on.

"Take the Ark and we shall lead you to the next corridor" said the Cherub again. "We must hurry and you must remove the Ark from this room"

Several of the cherubs flew upwards and pulled the chariot representing the moon backwards. This chariot had been slowly circling the saucer that rested above the wrestlers in the fountain. As they pulled backwards on the chariot the stone dolphin in the corner of the fountain closest to the box seats began to lower itself downward into the fountain. The water began to drain out of the fountain and shortly afterwards the fountain stopped flowing water all together.

"Hurry! Templars take the Ark and exit though the fountain's hidden stairway," said the voice of the Cherub.

The inside of the fountain was deep. It was about ten to twelve cubits deep and at the corner where the dolphin had submerged there was the beginning of a stair leading down into the fountain.

"What about our dead brother?" Adsideo asked the Cherub.

"He has been taken already," Said the Cherub.

They looked around and saw that Dominic was gone!

"Where is his body?" Adsideo yelled.

"Do not worry. You shall see your brother again," said the voice.

"Where will this lead us?" asked Adsideo.

"To your destiny" answered the Cherub "now you must leave. May God be with you"?

Several of the Cherubs began to flutter their wings and usher the Templars towards the fountains hidden stairway. Maurice led the way as they began down the stairs. Sylvester and Arminius carried the rear of the Ark, while Democritus and Colin were at the head of the men carrying the Ark. Adsideo and Laurence made up the rear of the group.

They reached the bottom of the fountain floor and saw the Dolphin, which had lowered itself, and they then saw that there was a doorway, which was behind the bottom of the stairs. Maurice signaled to the others to stop while he looked through the portal. He pulled his head back and signaled for them to follow him as he continued through the doorway.

"Laurence you and Arminius see about leading the animals down the stairs" Adsideo said.

"I do not think this will be possible. The steps are wet and they will slip" Arminius replied.

Laurence walked back to the top of the staircase and saw that the cherubs were cradling the first of the horses in one of the tapestries and began lifting it upwards. The cherubs flew the animal down to the bottom of the fountain floor. As soon as one animal was landed then another was being flown in by another set of the cherubs until all ten of the animals were led into the doorway below the fountain stairway.

"We are grateful to you" Laurence said to the cherubs as the last of them flew upwards from the fountain floor.

The cherubs flew back up to the wall mantels and did not utter a word of reply.

They all entered into a large chamber and as soon as Laurence entered through the door opening it slammed closed. Then the sound of water could be heard, through the door, splashing onto the floor of the fountain.

"It was a trick!" yelled Sylvester.

"Run!" said Arminius.

"No, stay calm" Adsideo yelled at them both "It was not a trick. They gave us back the Ark. Do not be fools. Calm down!"

"They are trapping us down here! Said Arminius "we will not escape"

"Calm down! Arminius Calm down, we will be all right!" said Adsideo.

"He is right, Arminius. We will be all right. The Ark is on its way to God! Remember our mission!" said Laurence.

"What about Dominic?" said Arminius "he is not all right!"

"Of course he is, we will see him soon. Remember what the Cherubs said" Maurice added to the conversation.

"Just trust in them and in your faith," said Sylvester.

The water filling the fountain room could hardly be heard now. There was a sudden pause in the Templars conversation. Then Maurice said "Come on, let's get moving"

They walked the horses through the room, which was surrounded in huge statues of men along the walls. They were about six cubits high and each had different dress of Armor and helmet. They all carried a sword in one hand and a scroll or tablet in the other hand. There were differences in their ethnicity and facial features. They all had things in common and differences as well. At the top of each was a hollowed out space in the wall, which had iron flat strapping woven over them. Behind these cages were fires burning. At the feet of each of the figures there were large saucers filled with water and flowers. This filled the room with a sweet fragrance.

In between each of the statues were alcoves; in these were a bench and a table. On the tables were a shelf with a candle sitting on it. Each candle was burning and there was additional light proved by a wall sconce inside.

The main ceiling was high but the alcoves ceilings were low and the openings were arched. The walls inside seemed to be covered in soot from the burning lamps.

"This room is very interesting," said Laurence "would anyone mind if I look around a bit"

"Is there something that you find interesting about this place" asked Maurice.

Maurice thought about Laurence at the dining room table. He could not forget about this and was suspicious of his old friend.

"I do not know anything you do not know. And yes I do find this room interesting" Laurence said as he stepped down from the saddles stirrups.

"What do you see that has your interest?" asked Arminius.

"Scrolls, writings" said Democritus as he got off of his horse as well.

"You stay together" Adsideo ordered them all.

"Aye" Sylvester said, "I agreed that we should search this room to find a way out"

"All right but, stay in groups" said Adsideo.

"I will stay with you. If you do not mind," said Colin who had been silent through the conversations.,

"I do not mind" Adsideo replied.

"Arminus and I will search together," said Sylvester "Maurice who will you go with?"

"I will stay and feed the horses" Maurice replied.

"We too will help with the horses" said Adsideo as he looked at Colin and then back to Maurice. "I do not want to lose sight of the Ark," said Adsideo.

Laurence walked toward one of the alcoves and picked up a scroll that was on the shelf and then sat it on the table. He unrolled it and saw that it was written in the hieroglyphics that they had seen through out the subterranean rooms and passages. Below the glyphs was a written language that he recognized as the Hebrew written language. He began to read this and soon found himself reading aloud to the others.

"In the year one thousand-four hundred and fifty-one since creation. I find that my duties for the Lord are not complete, as my peers believe they are. I

find myself sitting here in this room with no visible way
out. No way to complete my journey. I dare not to turn
back and take a return trip through the corridors from
which I came. The peril from which I came could only
be managed though by faith and in my current situation
I do not know if I have the strength. Nor do I know if I
have the faith to complete this journey much less to
repeat the one from which I have just passed.

There is a stone door blocking my way and when
I try to listen through the wall I think I hear the slight
sound of water running" Laurence read and was
fascinated by the writing. It seemed to him that this person
that wrote this was very well versed in both languages and
they were beautifully written. Laurence told the others that
the "the rest of this is a story or diary of someone trapped in
this room for some length of time" The others had stopped
what they were doing so that they could listen to Laurence
read.

"That sounds very intriguing," said Adsideo "but
we need to move on"

"Let us set up a camp and listen to Laurence read
the rest of this story," said Democritus "besides I bet the all
of us would like to rest as well"

"Alright, we will feed and water the horses, then
ourselves. If Laurence wants to read to us then I guess we
will have to feed him too" Adsideo as he smiled slightly to
the others. "Laurence, help me unpack the horses first and
then you can read. The rest of you unload the Ark and start
a fire," Adsideo told them while turning back to the horses.

"You heard the man. Let's unpack and then we can
listen to Laurence read," said Democritus.

"I would feel better if we just got some rest and
then left this room. I do not like it here. It is creepy," said
Colin.

They all seven began unloading and preparing a fire. They unloaded the Ark and said a blessing to the Lord as they made a bread and wine offering to him.

"Laurence, we will begin preparing the meal while you read. Then you will have the first watch. Then while you sleep I will take the next watch," said Democritus.

"Does not sound like you are doing me any favors" Laurence replied.

"Someone had to do it," said Sylvester.

Laurence walked back to the alcove and sat at the table. He unrolled the scroll once again and picked up where he had left off at before.

"When I listen through the wall I also hear the sounds of women talking and sometimes I think I hear laughing" Laurence looked over to the others and then back down to the scroll. **"I do not know what purpose I serve the Lord at this time. I have not heard a spoken word for weeks now. When I speak to myself I feel as if someone besides the Lord is listening but not even he will answer,"** Laurence continued to read these words. **"I having thought that I had served my Lord as best as could be expected but, now only to learn or assume that I am being punished. For what, I do not know. I have passed from life in front of my peers only to awaken to this series of grand halls and chambers such as this one. After several days in this one I believe this will be the last room in my journey. I await news from my Lord and will save my quill until then"**

Laurence rolled up the scroll and sat it back in its place on the table. He pulled out another from the shelf and opened it and began to read from it. He did not read aloud because he found that it was a duplicate of the first. He pulled another of the many on the shelf to find they were each the same as the first.

"They are all the same," Laurence said to the others.

"Why would anyone make this many copies of this letter?" Adsideo asked as he looked to Laurence and then the others.

"I do not know but this is only one of many such alcoves and manuscripts" Laurence replied to them all. "Well let's look though them," Maurice said to them quickly.

"Are there any others among us besides myself that cannot speak the written words" Sylvester asked the others.

"I can read," said Arminius.

"So can I" said Colin.

"I can too" said Adsideo.

"I cannot," said Maurice.

"I can," said Democritus.

"Alright, Sylvester and Maurice, you two watch the Ark and the horses. The rest of us will look through the writings," Adsideo ordered.

They fanned out to separate rooms and began opening the scrolls only to find that each were copies of the first. None of them took time to restore the scrolls to their original state. They left the alcoves in disorder as they went from one to the other.

They gathered at the opposite end of the room.

"This is insane! Who would do such a thing as this?" said Democritus.

"Apparently someone with a lot of time to spare" Laurence replied.

"The author did say he was going to lay down the quill until hearing from the Lord" added Adsideo.

"Well, I say we have a closer look around," said Colin "there is always more then what there appears to be around here"

"Did anyone notice that there was something strange about the candles on the tables?" asked Laurence.

"That the wax does not melt or burn?" Adsideo said weakly.

"That is the way I see it," said Laurence "maybe Colin is right"

"Then let us have another look around," said Adsideo.

"Why don't me and Democritus look around and the rest of you go back and stay with Sylvester and Arminius. We will yell at you if you are needed or if we find anything important," Laurence said to them.

"Why don't you go on back to the camp and look after the Ark?" Colin asked Adsideo "I would like to stay here and help Laurence and Democritus look for a way out of here and the scroll has me baffled by its origin and I would also like to know who the author is."

"Very well" Adsideo said to them as he and Maurice headed back to the other end of the room to meet up with Sylvester and Arminius.

"I hope they hurry because I am tired now so I cannot imagine how they will feel once they get back to the camp" Maurice said to Adsideo.

"Do not worry about them. I will feel much better when I have the Ark in my sights once again" Adsideo said as they continued to walk back to the camp.

"How shall we go about our search this time" Colin asked Laurence.

"First of all we never finished the first search and second of all there were some things that I have already noticed that may make all of the difference to our search" said Laurence rather sharply as if he had been offended by Colin's remark.

"I did not mean to make you angry with me. I only wanted to show my enthusiasm" Colin replied, as he looked Laurence in the eye.

"Do not push your rich boy attitude on me" Laurence said as he bowed his chest out and came closer to Colin.

"I do not know what is happening here but it will stop, now!" said Democritus "stop this unimportant gibberish. I see that it will take an adult to conquer this room so both of you had better sit down"

"I will search on my own," Colin said as he walked away from them and towards the farthest center alcove at their end of the huge room. The statues at this end of the room were of a Norseman's costume or dress. They each held different hilted broad swords. These were almost familiar to Colin but he could not say that he had ever seen these three creatures before now.

He thought maybe at first that they were like the ones at some of the plays that he used to see during the Maydays of his youth. He remembered the green Robin festivals and the tales of how the name Robinson was given to some of the children. He could not pin point a time that he had seen these three Norsemen before. He stopped for a moment and looked at the faces caved out of the solid rock. He looked back towards Laurence and Democritus. They appeared to stand there speaking to each other. He shook his head and then turned in the direction of the three statues and he began to walk away once more.

As Colin approached the first of the rooms he noticed that they were all painted the same color and the tables and chairs all matched each other. He stopped again and this time he looked to either side of the room he was standing in and then towards the rooms on each side of him. They were all just like each other. The scrolls on each shelf was stacked and placed like the other. He had never noticed this as they were searching each of the rooms before as a group. Maybe this is what Laurence meant when he had gone off on him about the sharp remark.

Colin began to walk into the first room. It was the center one of the three rooms at his side of the great room and he noticed that the huge stone feet of the statue, which sat to his left, had a sailor's sandals on while the one to the right had infantry footwear. So it seemed that this was a military symbol? He entered the room and pulled the chair from the table. He pulled the scrolls down and sat them in a pile to his left. He then opened the first of these and began to read. It began as the first reading of the scrolls had. He was not discouraged by this and continued to read it. He was looking for any noticeable difference in the wording or descriptions, even a change in the writing. There did not appear to be any differences as he continued to read. He noticed that the glyphs were the same but the ink color was different than the first search had revealed. He began to look through the pile of scrolls to see if there were any differences in the ribbons, which tied them together. There was not. He looked back down to the one, which was opened in front of him. He continued to read the last of the manuscript and then rolled it up and set it on his right hand side.

Colin reached over to the stack of scrolls on his left side when he heard Laurence and Democritus speaking to each other. He looked out of the alcove and he could see Democritus as he followed Laurence into one of the Alcoves to the right side of the room he sat in. the room they entered was several rooms down from him.

He could hear them speaking to each other as they began to search the room.

"There has to be one of the rooms different from the others. I mean there has to be a trick door somewhere. According to the writing, the Author came in from the opposite direction then we did," said Laurence.

"The problem is finding the other direction," Democritus said.

"Well, since we came in from down that way. I thought we would begin at this end. Just stop doubting and start looking" Laurence answered.

Colin heard them as they rustled around in the room. He began to look at the pile of scrolls at his right hand side. He picked up another and began to open it up and lay it over the one he had already been looking at when he had heard Laurence and Democritus.

He heard Laurence groan and Democritus yelled "pull on it Laurence!" then the sound of stones grinding. Then there was silence.

Colin listened for a moment then jumped to his feet with the scroll still in his hand and ran to the room that he had seen Laurence and Democritus enter. Once he reached it, he looked in it rather quickly and passed on to the next room then back again since they were both empty.

Colin ran into the room, which he thought that they had entered and looked at the walls and then at the table. He did not see anything unusual at all. None of the scrolls appeared to be disturbed from the shelf that they sat on. He glanced to his right and then left while he looked at the edges of the walls. Then he began to look at the flooring. He saw nothing unusual from the other rooms. He turned back towards the door opening when he noticed that the only footprints in the dusty room were his own. "What the..." Colin thought to himself as he suddenly reached down to move the candle from the table. The entire room rotated and he was now facing another rooms back wall. He looked at the room's walls and then walked forward.

"Laurence? Democritus? Where are you?" Colin whispered "hey!" "Where are you?" He yelled this time.

"We are over here!" he heard Democritus say as he waved a small fire of some kind in the air in front of him.

"Come and look over here," Democritus yelled to Colin.

Colin could see that Laurence was moving stones or some other objects in the shadows of the right hand corner from where he stood. "There is sunlight through here! We see sunlight!" Laurence yelled as his face lit up with the light.

Colin could see the light on Laurence's face from where he stood and began to walk towards his fellow Guards. He looked at the floor and saw the gleam on the floor, which revealed a preferred and worn path.

Where there had been an effigy of a pair of cobras entangled with each other was now a hole with light streaming through it.

"What do you see on the other side of the wall?" Colin asked Laurence as he reached them.

"I can see another room" Laurence said aloud "there are statues lining the wall"

"We should return to the camp and tell the others," said Democritus.

"Wait, let us find out more about what we are going to tell them about first" Laurence said abruptly.

"I think we should listen to Democritus" Colin said in response to Laurence's statement.

"I did not ask what you thought," Laurence answered, "We will continue onward"

"No we will not!" Colin shouted at Laurence "we will go and get the Captain and the others"

"I will go with you" Democritus said to Colin "Laurence, you should stay here in case we cannot get the room to rotate. We might need your help in returning to this room"

"If you return and I am not here then think nothing of it, for I will have gone ahead of you," Laurence said aloud to the both of them.

"You should wait on us," Democritus told Laurence, "we are stronger as a group"

"Then the two of you should go! I will do as you ask and wait for you but do not waste anytime. Return as fast as you can for I will not wait forever. Once you see in the room of the light you will understand the power and desire," Laurence told the two of them as he sat against the wall and lowered his head.

"You should rest" Democritus replied to him "wait on us and get some rest" Democritus took a portion of bread from his pouch and handed it to Laurence.

Democritus told Colin they should be on their way as they headed back to the wall with the alcove room and stepped inside. There was a lever that had to be pulled downward next to the opening to the alcove. Colin pulled it downward and they rotated back to the room, which they had come from. They began toward the camp, which was at the other end of the room.

Chapter Twelve

Adsideo had been asleep and awoke to Sylvester and Arminius speaking with each other about Democritus slaying Desiree.

Adsideo sat up and then stood to his feet. He began to walk towards the horses to find his wineskin of water. He wanted to wash his face.

"The Captains awake" Sylvester said aloud for all to hear.

"Wake the others. We should find Laurence and the other two"

Maurice was the only other brother asleep and was easily awoken by Arminius's gentle kick, which almost cost him his foot.

"Put the dagger away! I am not meaning you any harm," Arminius said as he laughed and walked back towards where Sylvester still stood.

"Let us two go in search of Laurence, Democritus, and Colin "Sylvester said to Adsideo "this way we will not need to load the animals so soon"

Adsideo was about to agree to this when Democritus and Colin approached the camp.

"Where is Laurence?" Maurice asked them before they could even reach the camp.

"Let us have some water and rest and then we will tell you the way out of this room and where Laurence is at" Democritus told them.

Democritus and Colin sat down and drank water and began to tell Adsideo and the others about the rotating alcove room at the other end.

"Which room was it that did this" Maurice asked.

"It was the third room from the last. On the left side, at the other end of this room. You will need to step inside and rotate the candleholder. Then the other room will be revealed." Colin explained to them as he sat there very tired and wearily.

"Alright, you two rest for a few minutes longer and then we can go to Laurence" Adsideo said in response.

"Have some bread" Arminius said to Democritus "you too Colin"

"It will give you strength as well," Maurice said as he pulled down a bedroll for each of them and placed them behind their heads.

"We are not sleeping!" Colin said loudly "we must hurry back to Laurence"

Sylvester, who had entered the nearest of the Alcoves to them, turned the candleholder and spun out of sight as that room rotated into another room. This room contained what appeared to be enough armor to supply a very large army. The armor all of which was polished bright and shiny was arraigned and stacked in various sizes.

Sylvester turned towards the armor and stepped from the alcove room. As he stepped over the rotate able floor he saw the lever, which would reset the room to its previous place. It was on the sidewall. He pulled it and stepped back into the alcove quickly as it returned him to his group.

"Did you see Laurence?" Colin asked Sylvester.

"No, just a room full of Armor and weaponry" Sylvester replied.

"The room that Laurence is in is on the opposite side of this room anyway!" said Democritus.

"He is right," said Colin.

"Try a room on this side," Colin said to Sylvester, as he pointed toward their left side.

"I will try the next room," Arminius said.

Arminius stepped into the room nearest them to the left and once inside it he then grabbed the candleholder and the room rotated as expected. Inside he saw a room full of jewels and treasures he had not seen since the inventories of their late King Salomon. His eyes opened wide as the gleaming gems, polished silver, and gold let off a stream of light. He walked out of the alcove and over to the first of many chests that filled the room. There were also great heaps of pearls, precious gems, and gold vessels of all types lying on the floor of this room. Arminius was amazed and picked up an amulet with a gold necklace and stuck it in his pocket.

He thought he should return to the others quickly. He stepped back over the threshold to the alcove room and pulled the lever to reset the room. He was facing the others, they each were standing in the same place they had been before he had moved the candleholder.

"This room was filled with unimaginable riches! Gold, silver, pearls, and Gems," shouted Arminius to the others as he reentered their room.

"We should search all of these rooms before we leave" said Sylvester.

"We do not have time for that!" shouted Democritus "why will you not listen to us. Laurence told us he would not wait for us for very long"

"I forgot, I am sorry!" said Sylvester.

"We should be going soon" said Adsideo to Maurice "let the two of them rest for a few more minutes and then we will be on our way"

"I will take Sylvester and load the Ark and the camp goods" Maurice replied.

So the camp and all of the goods along with the Ark were loaded and they began on their way. It was only a few minutes ride and they were there at the alcove that had led them to the room of light.

"This is it," said Colin "let me and Democritus go in first"

"I will go with you," said Maurice "Adsideo you and the others should stay with the Ark to keep it under guard"

"Good thinking" said Adsideo in agreement.

The three entered the alcove room and moved the candleholder. They were once again whished away.

"Hey, let us look in these rooms next to us while we await the others" said Sylvester.

"No we will wait here for them" Adsideo said "we will not be off on some other adventure while there could be danger about"

"He is right and you should not be eaten up with greed," said Arminius to Sylvester.

"I am not eaten up with greed" Sylvester replied quickly "I will attest to being eaten by adventure and curiosity though"

"Well what ever you call it you will need to listen to the Captain," said Arminius.

"Settle this now!" Adsideo said with a shout "stop the bickering right now"

They all three fell silent for a moment. Then they all turned their heads towards the alcove room that their brothers had entered into. "Let one us step inside at a time with one horse until all of them are though and then I will follow last" Adsideo told the others.

"I will go first and get the others to help manage the animals while I return the room to you each time" said Sylvester.

Sylvester reached for the horse that Adsideo had been leading that was carrying the Ark first but Adsideo pulled the reins away and spoke very sternly as he told Sylvester that "this horse will come though last with me"

Arminius pulled his horse over to the alcove and asked that it go through with Sylvester.

Sylvester pulled the horse into the cramped space and then pulled the candleholder. The room rotated around to reveal the next room. He then stepped onto the path and saw the light streaming through the wall, which was now an opening that before had been bricked up solid. The rubble still lay on the floor next to the opening. Sylvester walked towards the opening with the horse in tow when he remembered that the other Templars should have been there to meet him. They were nowhere to be seen.

"Democritus! Laurence! Colin! Maurice! Where are you?" he yelled as he continued to approach the opening. He could not hear anything other than the sounds of the horse and his own footsteps echoing throughout the room.

There was a sudden shiver down his spine as a cool breeze passed him as he came near the opening. The horse became spooked by this and began to backup and whinnied repeatedly. It was all he could do to hang onto the reins as he spun around to control the horse.

Sylvester became spooked he and ran with the horse still in tow into the alcove. He reached over and pulled the lever to reset the room.

He returned to the room to see Adsideo and Arminius standing right in front of him with the horses in a line. Sylvester fell over with his hands on his knees and put his head down. He was breathing heavily and his face as white as combed fleece.

"What happened in there?" Adsideo asked, "Where are the others"

"I did not see the others," Sylvester answered in between gasps. "Let us all go one after the other as I said before" Sylvester continued "except one will have to go and receive the animals, one to transfer them, and Adsideo to load the horses from this room. The horses need to be contained in the next room while all of this takes place."

"Do as he says" Adsideo told Arminius.

Arminius let the first of the horses into the alcove and then pulled the candleholder. Once he was on the other side of the wall he pulled the lever and reset the room to return to Adsideo and Sylvester. Then as quickly as he sent it off there was Sylvester with the next horse until finally

Adsideo joined them with Dominic's horse, which now carried the Ark of the Covenant.

"There is the opening into the next room," said Sylvester to the others.

"Come on let's get this over with and find the others quickly" Adsideo ordered them.

So as ordered Sylvester and Arminius tied all of the horses to each other's and began to lead them towards the opening in the wall. The light streaming through was a long time coming to them. It had been a while since they had seen what appeared to be sunlight. They squinted their eyes as they approached the opening. Adsideo followed last in line with the Ark. Sylvester lead them through the opening first with three of the horses followed by Arminius and his four horses and then Adsideo and Dominic's horse. The Mules followed behind even though they were not tied to the other animals.

Once inside the next room the view was unbelievable to them as their eyes saw its grandeur for the first time. There were more of the huge statues as were in the library room of alcoves but these were much taller and were made entirely of gold. They had brass overlay to define clothing and armor.

The light that they had seen from the opening in the wall was streaming from the ceiling. It came through a skylight that was made from a clear-cut stone that was transparent.

There was also round windows lighting each end of the rectangle room, which they stood in one end of.

There were two rows of columns that ran the length of the room and a huge fountain in the center. The fountain was large but simple in design. There was one single ornamented column, which supported a saucer which water bubbled through the center of. The water flowed over the edges of the saucer and ran down the column into the pool below. The walls of which stood above the floor line by at least two cubits and was topped with a carved white marble fence and columns.

The sidewalls of the room to either side were lined with the huge gold statues that were approx forty to fifty cubits high and stood ceiling to floor in their stance. Not a one of them sat, all were standing in their casts of gold representation.

As in the previous rooms these statues appeared to be from many different cultures and eras. Some of these Adsideo recognized but may of these he did not.

Though the room was rectangle shaped it was very wide in its distance from sidewall to sidewall. They could not see the farthest wall from them clearly due to the great distance between it and them. All of the floors, walls, and ceiling were constructed of the white marble that they had seen in the corridor.

They stood and marveled in the warm sunlight and bathed in its brightness. They were speechless due to the warmth.

Sylvester began to slowly walk towards the center of the room.

It appeared that the horses wanted water more than Sylvester wanted to walk to the fountain. Arminius was watching Sylvester and then looked back to Adsideo who nodded to him to venture forward. Arminius did as signaled and was followed by Adsideo.

The light that showered down from the skylight was amazing. Adsideo knew now that they had somehow come out above ground. As they passed the huge white marble columns, Adsideo looked up and noticed for the first time the plants, which hung around all of the upper sections of the columns and perimeter of the walls.

They continued onward towards the fountain and found that there was a lower trough wall surrounding the fountain, which was fed by waterspouts coming from the fountain wall. The water shot through the mouths of golden dolphins. They were evenly spaced around the fountain. There were at least fifty of these dolphins surrounding the wall of the fountain.

Sylvester untied the horses and allowed them to drink water.

"Water them quickly and lets get going. The others must be up ahead," said Adsideo.

Arminius untied his horses and joined Sylvester at the trough.

"I have not heard a sound in this room other than the water from this fountain and our own foot steps" Arminius said to Sylvester.

"Do you think the others have left this room?" Sylvester asked in response to Arminius.

"We shall soon find out!" said Adsideo as he came walking up behind them.

"If you have questions than let us discuss them together," Adsideo added to his comments.

"I did not mean anything by this. It was only to gather another opinion from a friend" said Sylvester.

"Well let's try to keep all communications to include all members" Adsideo told them both. "Come on, we need to catch up to the others" he added.

They pulled the horses together as before and then resumed their journey towards the opposite side of the room. The horse's hooves could be heard echoing through out the room.

"So much for a chance on hearing anything ahead of us before it hears us" Adsideo stated.

As they passed the columns they could see the statues that lined the walls, one after the other.

They marched on as they watched all around themselves for the unexpected. All seemed peaceful as they marched to the other end of the room. As they neared the last row of columns they could make out a raised level in the floor and what appeared to be a throne ahead of them.

Adsideo could not believe his eyes, for what he saw was unbelievable. Behind it were tapestries of gold weave. Centered behind the throne was a set of doors that were Identical to the tabernacle doors leading to God's house in Jerusalem. How did these get here he thought to himself. Why, even the wall carvings behind the throne were the same as in the tabernacle.

Arminius having seen this immediately looked up to the ceiling and saw that embedded in the ceiling and in the skylight was the constellations of the night sky.

"I have been in this room before" said Arminius to the others "in a dream I had, remember Adsideo, I told you of this"

"So the dreams continue to come true for the both of us" Adsideo replied.

"Well let's see what is to be seen" Sylvester said to the two of them.

"Very well" said Adsideo.

They continued toward the raised floor area and began up the steps when suddenly there was a sound like a clap of thunder that nearly deafened them all. Then from the ceiling area there formed a red cloud which lightning could be seen shooting to the floor, and then another clap of thunder. This cloud lowered itself to just above the throne and then descended.

The three men fell backwards down the steps. They got up, turned back to the steps and faced the raised floor. The animals began to whinny and pulled away from the Templars. They ran to the other end of the room.

Then there before there eyes appeared a man sitting upon the throne. He was dressed in a white linen wrap. He had a long beard and shoulder length hair. They could not make out the color of his hair or the features of his face. This was due to the light that was emitting from his body.

His feet appeared to be made of the pure essence of light. This light was so bright that none of the three Templars could stand to look directly at his face.

The wall behind the throne which, housed the Tabernacle doors and the Tapestries, arched high to the ceiling above. In the upper center section was one of the circular windows. This was made with colored glass and had a trio of angels inset in it. Two were descending and one in an upward flight.

Above the angels was a throne with the same man, which sat in front of them now. The rising angel held one out stretched arm towards the sitting figure. In the hand of this angel was one of the sacred tablets and the other tablet was in the angels folded arm held tightly to its side. This angel was dressed in a white tunic with gold trim. His head was encircled in a crown of gold leaves.

The two descending angels were different from the ascending angel as well as each other. One was dressed in black and held a whip in one hand, which was pulled over its head as if ready to strike, while the other hand was doubled up in a fist and held lightning bolts.

The second descending angel was dressed in red and had a crown of roses on his head and in his hands was a book and a quill.

Below the descending angels was a mass of humans and animals that seemed to be in chaos and all of their eyes were transfixed on the descending angels. Some appeared to be jubilant while the others attempted to hide from the angel's sight.

The Templars became transfixed on the vision in glass and the light that was streaming though it. When suddenly a voice spoke which was so deafening that it knocked them all incoherent.

Adsideo, who had fallen straight down to the floor with his hands covering his ears, looked up towards the throne with hopes of mercy and saw the figure as it stood and began to walk towards him. Adsideo began to withdraw from further harm by wrapping his arms over his head and then pulling himself into a fetal position.

Then he heard the voice. It was the voice he had heard before. The voice of God. The same voice he had overheard so many times before while in service of King Solomon.

Adsideo then looked up in to the light and saw his face.

He appeared concerned and sorrowful yet pleased to see them.

"Come and stand before me, all of you," he said to the three of them. "Bring the Ark and present it to me and your task will end with a new beginning" he then turned and began to walk back to the throne and sat down. The brightness subsided a great deal as for the first time they were able to make out the entire form, which God had chosen to reveal himself as.

"Adsideo, this is not the form that I chose. This is the form that was given to me. Just as I gave you form, as the form of your Fathers, so is mine. Now go and bring me the Ark"

The three of them turned around and walked towards the horses, which had returned to their end of the room. The horses now seemed serene as an animal could ever be.

Adsideo and Arminius began to untie the bindings from the Ark that held it to Dominic's horse, while Sylvester pulled the poles from the side of his horse.

Sylvester pushed the poles though the rings of gold on the Ark.

Adsideo and Arminius picked up either end of the Ark and lifted it from the horses back and began carrying it towards the throne.

Sylvester followed closely behind Arminius, who made up the rear of the Ark, as they proceeded up the steps to the throne. Once they reached the top of the throne platform they sat it on the marble floor. They all three kneeled to the floor and began to praise God for there safe return to him.

"Adsideo, bring your men and stand before me. Do not fear me, I have given you this great task and you have fulfilled it. Now it is time to return the Ark to me and be rewarded" God then stood up in front of his throne and with his raised arms motioned for them to come closer to him.

"You have shown your valiant bravery and dedication towards me" God began "you shall be rewarded as promised. Because you and the others have shown your faith in me, and your judgment in the situations you endured to return the Ark to its final resting place. I shall grant you eternal life and you shall never suffer loss of life by injury, illness, or mortal wound. You shall, depending on personality, have the ability to change the fate of the people. This can be accomplished by two methods, which must always be monitored. First and foremost, your responsibilities will be to prevent the completion of Bellabezzer's plan to defeat Light and all things that are good.

The second responsibility will be to keep the people reminded of my love for them and their responsibilities to me"

Adsideo looked up to God and wanted to ask a question but as he saw the opportunity to speak God began to speak once more.

"Adsideo, I know better than you about my great design. It does not matter that none of you are of Abraham's bloodline but you are of Noah's blood.

It is the reason I chose you, that you were all of innocent peoples. For the love of all people I do not wish to destroy the earth ever again. Even after granting every wish to the people of Abraham for laws and now Kings they still disappoint me by their sins. I shall send a Savior to the people in time but until then, your Templars shall keep a guard over your fellow man and keep them morally gracious to their fellow man. Love, Honor, loyalty, Duty, Grace, Wisdom, fair in heart and stern in judgment, these shall be your virtues. And the most important virtue shall be the Truth, for it alone shall reign over the wicked."

Adsideo again looked up and wanted to speak but did not.

Then God motioned for Adsideo to step forward, and he did so.

"Speak to me as you wish" said God.

"Our mighty God" Adsideo said as he began to speak "we have seen many times over in our meager lives, that the strong and wicked prevailed over the true and weak"

"That has been true in the past on occasion but, you shall learn that the truth shall cast a light on the guilty from which they cannot hide" replied God.

"But now, with you eight Templars, I shall have a protector for the peoples morals, love, and respect for their fellow man.

Some of the angels have been granted this duty before and could not complete the task. Before I flooded the earth I relieved them of this duty and have not filled that position since. Until now that is. I have faith that you can fulfill this duty?"

"Oh, we most certainly will try our best" Adsideo replied "but Lord we lost one member due to his death and the other four were separated from us and now there only remains us three"

"Do not worry, Dominic and the others will be joining you in this palace very soon" said God "they have all been given the choice to be rewarded before you arrived. They all accepted the duty"

"Oh, as usual we are the last to arrive" Arminius said without thinking.

"Aye, but you brought the Ark and will be given greater rewards," said God.

"The return of our brothers would be enough," said Sylvester.

"Oh, but you will have much more than that" said God "you will be able to know where evil lives in the minds of men at any given time. You will be able to feel the pain of the deceived. You shall have the ability to see the near future, but only the near future. You will also be able to move through time and space so that you can act upon this knowledge to prevent chaos"

"What will we do if we make a mistake?" asked Adsideo.

"Chose well your actions before acting upon premature conclusions. Do not let your years of observations disillusion your faith in mankind" God retorted.

"Could we go back in time and see our loved ones?" asked Sylvester.

"You can but' if you travel to the past you cannot be seen physically nor could you change the past to alter the future. If you go to the future you will be able to see the results of your past actions. In the present you can make changes to alter the future for good of the people."

"But how will we know what is right?" asked Adsideo.

"You shall decide so how can you be wrong?" God answered.

"But would we not be playing as God then?" asked Adsideo.

"Adsideo, I have a great tendency to destroy the sinner with terrible vengeance. I tell the people the way I expect them to live and they listen for a while. Then they revert back as they were. I do not have the patience to keep them from punishment.

You will not be able to do that but you may be more patient than I have become."

"I do not see how the three of us will be able to control all of mankind my Lord," said Arminius.

"You shall learn to" replied God "there will be the other five to help you. I told you that they were to join you but you shall direct them and all eight of you will spread out over the earth and influence all of mankind. Seek out your fellow man in all civilized countries and cities. There and only there will you be heard? Everywhere else shall you find the slow of wit and the ignorant.'

"If you do not find the civil people then you shall help them to develop to a higher love and respect for me, themselves and the others around them"

Adsideo spoke up "If you have this faith in us, like the faith we have in you then I shall speak for us all. I, Adsideo, shall nurture my fellow man from now until eternal life takes its last breath of air. Until the last heart beat on earth can be heard anywhere on this earth. Until you wish different from me I shall serve you to serve my fellow man," said Adsideo as he looked from God to Arminius and then Sylvester.

The two other Templars raised their arms into the air and the three of them gripped each other's hands and then released them with a yell.

"Then it will be said, that the Templars will be the judge and protectors of mankind for ever!" said God as he too raised his arm from his sitting position and said "The Templars! Guards over mankind"

"Why do we spread out around the civilized world? Would we not be more successful if we remained together as one larger force?" Sylvester asked.

"If you were to do that than the people would have to seek you out at one location" God explained to the three of them "If you were to spread out and then eventually bring them all together in peace you will find that your flock will be larger, also through your differences in ethnicity you could create a vast diversity of opinion and representation that would be far more reaching. You will also find it very hard to coexist with your fellow man should they were to find out about your immortality. So for this reason you will not be permitted to tell anyone, Ever!"

"What would happen should we fall in love or marry?" asked Adsideo.

"You can do any of these carnal acts but they must never know of your powers or immortality.

Marriage is not highly recommended but you may do as you desire" God answered.

"Lord, are we to be alone all of our existence?" Arminius asked.

"Only if you desire to remain alone, but I will be with you always" God answered.

"Live as though you were any other person. The only difference is that you will not be any other person. You are guardians, do not forget your duties"

"We understand" Adsideo said and he looked back at the other two Templars. They nodded in agreement to his statement.

"You shall not use your real names. No one should call you by your names other than when in the company of the other Templars. This way you will be able to fake your death under your alias as the generations pass on. After each mock death you should change your residence and region to avoid exposure," said God "if you are discovered or tell anyone than you will immediately stand before me. I will make sure of it! Other than this I will not judge you by your faults or your deeds."

"We understand" Adsideo said.

"Should you have a limb cut off and it is lost. Then you shall have a loss of limb and it will heal over.

If you keep the limb and realign it, it will heal up and you will have full use of it once again. It will have to have a dressing and kept clean for it to heal. A wound through the flesh will not bleed and will heal almost immediately.

Burns to the skin will not be suffered to you. Cold winds will not make you warm of blood. Not even a chill will you ever have from this day forth."?

"So we cannot feel?" asked Arminius.

"You will feel it but the weather will not harm you"

"We will be able to withstand any degree of heat?" Arminius asked again.

"Yes"-replied God.

"However you will only use these powers for what you believe in! Do it for good and not evil. If it is evil you use them for then you will suffer in the end. You have the fate of mankind in your interest, and then you will have my interest. I will not abandon you if you teach my word of love. Teach evil and you will learn evil like you cannot comprehend it at this time. You will stand before me for the last time" God continued to tell them.

"We understand," said Adsideo.

"You shall always know my feelings for what you do. I will not interfere, I will always be here for you to look to for guidance"

A light as bright as before began to shine from over Gods head and from this three angels slowly descended and landed on either side of God.

They were dressed just the same as the angels in the painted glass window that loomed over their heads.

The angel dressed in white on the right side of God and the angels in red and black were on the left side of God.

"This is Posterus" God said as he pointed to his right side.

"And this is Pridem and Nunc. Pridem in red and Nunc in black.

They will guard over the Ark. whoever should inquire of the Ark shall answer to them. For only those who can conquer these three angels shall they remove the Ark from this room?

This is the place from which the Ark was kept after the siege at Nebulas and whence King David removed it before Solomon brought it to the Tabernacle. So here it shall stay."

Pridem and Nunc took hold on either end of the poles to carry the Ark. Posterus lead them down the opposite side of the platform. They exited from the room though the Tabernacle doors and disappeared from sight.

"Remember your duties and obligations to man. You can now pass through the doors and you will find the other Templars waiting for you there"

God then vanished and the light level in the room returned to its original state.

Adsideo had not realized that this conversation would end this way, and so quickly. He had many more questions to ask. Then suddenly he heard a whispering voice. He looked at Arminius and Sylvester. They had both sat down on the floor. They both looked up to Adsideo and they seemed to be in shock.

Adsideo started to ask if they could hear the voice when he heard it clearly in his head as if it was his own thoughts.

"Adsideo, it is I, God. When you have solitude and prayer time I will answer your questions"

Then the voice was gone. He turned quickly towards the throne but it sat empty.

Adsideo turned back to the other two and he was smiling.

"Well lets find our brothers in the next room," said Adsideo.

"I am anxious to see Democritus as well as the others," added Sylvester.

"If I see Dominic in there I am walking straight up to him and kissing him" said Arminius.

They all began to laugh as they gathered the horses and started towards the Tabernacle doors.

Chapter Thirteen

From inside the room they could hear the sound of the lock or bolt being drawn. They approached the doors and heard a creaking sound come from the other side.

Then the doors opened swinging out towards them.

Pridem was the one pushing them open and for the first time they saw him this close and he began to speak, when Adsideo realized that he had been the man in his dreams.

"Come inside. We have been waiting for you." Pridem said to them with a smile on his face.

He turned back towards the doors as he had entered the throne room and now seemed prepared to close the doors once they were inside the Tabernacle.

They could hear the sounds of men laughing and having a good time. The sound of music and there were women here too. From the sounds they heard, they were having a very good time.

As they entered the room they saw that it was a great banquet room. There were two long tables that lined the walls to either side. There were tapestries hanging along the walls as well as various items of weaponry. The walls were of stone blocks, the floors terrazzo and the ceiling was very high and constructed with stone arching beams. They were sectioned symmetrically and a great chandelier hung in the center of each section. These were filled with row after row of oil burning lamps.

They could see at the opposite side of the room sat their brothers. They had all stopped their conversations and were looking back towards the new arrivals.

Maurice rose to his feet and shouted out a greeting to Adsideo.

"How very good it is to see you" he said "and the rest of our brothers are here too," he said to the other four Templars, which were sitting around him.

They sat on either sides of the table on the right hand side of the room. There sat Democritus, who had a very attractive woman sitting next to him, and next to them was Laurence. On the opposite side of the table were Maurice, Colin, and Dominic. All of who were sitting next to other attractive women.

"Dominic! How very good it is to see you," said Arminius.

Arminius then began towards the seated Templars and right up to Dominic as he had said he would. Arminius grabbed Dominic by both of his arms and kissed him.

The women seated there looked at the two men in surprise. Their eyes wide open.

Suddenly all of the men burst out laughing. As they did this, the women caught on to this spectacle and also began laughing.

"Well it is good to see you too," said Dominic as he wiped his mouth off with his right wrist.

"I never thought in a thousand years that I would see you again," said Arminius.

"None of us did," said Sylvester "but you seem in the best of health"

"Forever on" said Maurice as he grabbed a goblet from the table and raised it in toast to the others.

There appeared two other women into the dining area. They quickly poured Adsideo, Arminius, and Sylvester a goblet full of wine and motioned for them to sit at the table. They all raised their goblet into the air and Maurice continued his speech.

"For as far as we have come and for a far as we may go! I salute all of you for accepting me as your brother." Maurice said as he now sat back down next to the ebony skinned beauty at his side.

"Adsideo speak to us, you are our leader!" said Laurence aloud.

"Yes, speak to us," said Colin.

"All right, I will say to all of you that we have been given the greatest task in all of history and a responsibility that will never rest. I hope that you are all ready for this task and will remain pure in thought as you are in heart. I am very proud to say to anyone of you that I am glad to have had you at my side though out the protection and delivery of the Ark. I give you my alliance from now on. In times of crisis whether you call on me or not, I will be there for you," said Adsideo with his hand and goblet raised in the air. He turned and looked at each of his comrades as he spoke. After he stopped speaking, the others began to applaud him. They all stood and clapped until he would be seated. Adsideo could not do anything other than smile the whole time. He was with the ones who he knew he would have to trust with his secret life forever more.

They all sat down after Adsideo insisted. Once at the table together Adsideo asked the others to continue as they had before he arrived. There was a festive atmosphere about the room.

The girls began to dance to the music that seemed to come from nowhere. There were no musicians to be seen. This did not seem to interest any of the others for all of their eyes were on the young girls that danced before them.

There was an abundance of food on the table and more wine than should be allowed for one meal.

They were having a great time and were talking and laughing amongst themselves all most immediately.

"Let us make a pact with each other. On this day on every year let us come and meet. Then have a meal together!" said Democritus.

"That sounds like a great idea," said Adsideo "we should spend the end of a week together and we will then be able to align ourselves together for our common goal. To keep mankind from their own disaster"

"Shall we make the meeting place here?" asked Colin.

"No" said Adsideo "let us make it a different place each year"

"How will we know where to meet"? Asked Sylvester.

"By messenger" said Arminius "I shall give my services for this duty"

"That is a good thing for you to offer." Said Laurence "for that I will have to volunteer for the group as well"

"That will not be necessary. At least not yet any way" said Adsideo "you can offer your services for this as long as that is what you want to do. Should you ever tire from this task I am sure we can make other arraignments.

Each year a different one of us eight shall be the host for the dinner meeting. It will give us a chance to see the progress each has made on a eight year interval."

"All in favor of this say aye," said Democritus to the others "if you wish to disagree than say nay"

They all raised their hands and said "aye"

"The aye's have it," said Democritus.

"From now on I will not be your leader," said Adsideo.

This took all of the attention from the others and directed it towards Adsideo. Even the music stopped and all eyes were once again upon him.

"What do you mean you will not be our leader? Of course you will be! We would not have it any other way," said Maurice.

The others all said "aye" as they heard what Maurice had to say.

"From now on we are all as equal as the other next to him in ranks that is. We shall from now on share equally in the task which our lord has appointed us to."

"This is quite unexpected," said Sylvester.

"Yes it is" said Arminius in agreement to the statement.

"I will always be available to you as a brother but I will have a nation of my own to build, and this brings me to the next guideline for our committee. We shall never compete against each other. This must be promised"

"Aye" they all said aloud and almost at the same time.

"We should be able to trade freely with each other. This should also teach our fellow man the knowledge of brotherhood"

"Then is anything else that can be thought of at this time for our guidelines?" asked Laurence.

Suddenly there was a loud proclamation from Arminius.

"Look at the wall!" he said.

"How did this happen so quickly" said Democritus.

There on the wall behind them there was a great and fine detailed mural of the eight of them at this very room seated at this very table.

Then here in the banquet room, at the end of the table, stood the three guardian angels for the Ark.

Posterus began to speak to them "Templars let it be known that we shall never forget your dedication to our lord and the great task that you have achieved by removing the Ark from the hands of man and back into the hand of God. We shall never for one minute forget this. Now that we have carved this event into the wall. We shall always see it while in the service of our Lord, God"

"I believe this to be a good thing for all to see," said Adsideo "Especially the handsome carving of me"

"This cannot be allowed!" said Nunc "this place is to remain secret forever"

"Will we be allowed to come back here?" asked Arminius.

"No, you will not know how to get back here unless brought here by one of us," answered Pridem.

"You will each be in separate locations once you leave here" said Posterus "you will begin your new lives and service to the Lord"

"You may ask to return here and under some circumstances you may be allowed. This will have to come at the grace of God himself," said Nunc.

"Well I know at least I am the most handsome at this time so this makes me the most handsome man in history" said Colin.

"Well maybe there are others in the room who can decide this" said Maurice as be bumped Colin on the shoulder.

"Now please, let us be your hosts. Enjoy the food and the company but once you leave this room then you will be separated from each other. You shall know where to reach each other at all times and should communicate as much as possible" said Nunc.

"Please back to the festivities and have fun," said Posterus.

They all began to sit again as Adsideo and Arminius looked at each other for they knew there was something special ahead of them. All they could do at this time is wonder what it will be. Once they were free from here Adsideo planned on trying to use some of his new powers. Just to get to know them in case he would ever need them.

As they sat at the table he noticed that Maurice kept looking at him as if he was thinking about something. Adsideo then noticed though out the rest of the night that he would catch the others doing the same sort of thing. He even caught himself doing this a couple of times himself as he watched the others. Maybe they had known that after tonight they would not see each other for possibly a year.

They all continued to drink and eat as they watched the girls dance. There was a dark headed girl of Persian decent that Adsideo had his eye on during the night's festivities. She returned his favor to her looking back at him with short glances while she danced before them.

Soon Adsideo found himself beginning to feel sleepy. He asked Maurice where they were to sleep and was told that there was a door over to the left of the room as he pointed at it. There he was told was the grand hall and the offsetting chambering rooms.

"You will find everything in order" said Maurice "it is the best room I have ever sleep in"

"I think I will retire for the night. I have had a very interesting and eventful day today" said Adsideo.

"A very exciting month I would say," added Arminius to this conversation.

Adsideo stood up and walked towards the door. The Persian girl who had been dancing made a swirling maneuver towards Adsideo and landed right into his path. He caught her and held her arms. As if to help her catch her balance. As she stopped in front of him she looked up into his eyes and Adsideo saw something there. This was a look of hope that he saw in her eyes. Quickly he grabbed her and kissed her on the lips as though she would disappear in front of him without a moment to share together like this one.

"I see that you are as quick in love as you are in deep thought," said the Persian girl as she breathed in deeply.

"I do not know how long I will stay but I would like for you to visit with me for a while tonight" said Adsideo.

I would be honored to please the Captain in anyway needed," said the girl "my name is Dania" she said as she continued to look him in the eye as he did the same to her.

They were locked in this visual embrace for a moment when Adsideo thought about how tired he was again.

"I should be going to my chamber now, will you join me?" Adsideo asked.

"You go ahead. I will join you soon" she answered.

Adsideo continued on his original course and reached for the knob and opened the door. As he entered the hallway he saw that it was well lit and quite a bit wider than he would have built it. But never the less it was another beautiful room. There was a high ceiling with supporting beams and a set of lower beams, which were made of cedar timbers. Upon each of these beams sat some sort of planter with a draping flowering plant hanging over all edges of the planters. This made the smell of this room accented with there fragrances. There were paintings on wood slates aligning the hallway walls. There also were big oak doors that lined the walls of the hall. Most of the doors were open and as he walked up to the first couple of these doors that stood opposite each other. He could see that there were their names engraved in each of the doors. Each door had a different name of one of the Templars on it.

"This was very strange," he thought to himself.

Adsideo found that his chamber was at the very end of the hallway. It was centered in the end wall of the hallway. He walked into the room and saw that he had a corner room, which had two windows in it that looked out over a valley. The place that they were in seemed to be sitting atop a mountain. One of these windows opened out onto a balcony, which Adsideo walked out onto it.

The View was immaculate. He could not believe the spectacle before his eyes. Now granted that he had not seen the outside world for some time, it did not make a difference.

How could he ever get back to this place he thought to himself as he remembered what the angel had said earlier in the banquet room. The valley and surrounding mountains were unforgettable with there rugged but divine structuring.

"I will never forget this for the rest of my life" Adsideo told himself as he stood in the last light at dusk. The sun was beginning to set over the mountains. This view was directly in front of Adsideo as he looked off of the balcony. There were animals of all kinds to be seen in the trees below.

As he was looking off of the balcony he looked straight down the side of the palace structure. He saw that the wall line was straight down and he could not see if there were any doors below on this side of the palace. He could see that it was a long, long way down. He could not clearly see the pavement below.

Adsideo turned around and headed back into the chamber room and saw that there was a bath over in one corner. And best of all, there was hot water in it. He could see the wisps of steam as it evaporated off of the water. There was some kind on flowers floating on the top of the water.

This interested Adsideo Quite a bit for he knew that he smelt of sweat and the water would have to feel good about now.

As he walked over to the tub he heard the door to his chamber shut. He looked over and saw that Dania was standing there at the door. In her arms was a flat basket that she had linens in.

"Here let me undress you Master," she said as she approached Adsideo.

"I can manage if there are other things that you need to do. Like join me in the bath" Adsideo said to her.

"How about I bath you," she said as she sat the linens down on the bedding. "I have had my bath today" she added to the conversation.

"Have it your way then" Adsideo said to her as he began to disrobe him self.

As he took off his armor and then his clothing, Dania saw the many scars on his back and on his arms. Adsideo' s loincloth hit the flooring and he was in the bath as quickly as humanly possible. Maybe a little quicker for Dania thought for a moment that he had disappeared for a moment and then re-appearing in the tub.

She did not question her thoughts very long for she did not know of such things.

"Are you sure you will not join me" Adsideo asked her.

"I will be fine over here" she replied with a smile. She began to install the bedding and was fluffing pillows when Adsideo began to bathe himself.

The water felt very warm and relaxing to him as he laid his head backwards over the edge of the tub and closed his eyes. How comfortable he thought to himself.

Adsideo fell asleep and began to dream.

Back in the banquet hall the others were beginning to need rest as well. Colin had fallen asleep with his head on the table. Across the table from him was Dominic in the same shape, slumped over state of unconscious. There were two of the girl's servants that were trying to awaken them from their slumber. They were trying to take them into their chambers to sleep.

Maurice and Democritus were sitting up discussing the physical implications that were bound to arise by their influence on mankind in the possible future.

Laurence was up dancing with two of the girls and Sylvester was whispering in the ear of one of the two girls that was sitting on either side of him. She was giggling and laughing at whatever he was telling her.

Arminius sat alone and was thinking of some of the things that had been said to him and the others during the last few days. He thought of his village back on Dago. He thought of his grandfather Fein and all of the lands that they had once controlled. Could he make a difference there? He would have to wait to see. He thought that once they were to leave here he would go to Pelusium and hail a ship and sail back to Dago. Maybe he would find a Norse maiden to fill his bed with at night and his thoughts during the day.

Maurice stood from the table and spoke above the music and the others voices. Those that were awake that is.

"Let us clear the hall and seek the shelter of our bed chambers. Hopefully not alone" said Maurice "I am sure there will be adventure tomorrow" he said as he slightly slurred his words. They had all drank to much wine and were feeling very good.

The servants began to help the Templars off to their individual bedrooms where they would sleep tonight. Arminius was the last to stand from the table and had to help one servant get Colin to his room.

They bid each other a good night and retired to their rooms.

Chapter Fourteen

(Sylvester's story)

Sylvester woke up to the sound of running water and birdsong. He rolled over in the bed onto his side. He opened his eyes and saw through the marble window jambs, that his view was suddenly close enough to the ground that he was looking into the tree line. At first he did not think too much about it since his vision was still a little fuzzy from the amount of wine they had drank last night.

Then it dawned on him that something was different.

"Servant girl!" he shouted, "Where are you"

There was no answer. He listened carefully and then outside he heard people speaking! It was a language he had not heard in a long time but recognized it rather quickly. He then realized that his thoughts were in this language!

He could feel the thoughts of many people. Some were of distraught feels of pain and hope while others thoughts were of evil deeds. He had a very hard time trying to figure out what was being deciphered. His thoughts had to slow down for him to understand what was being said and by whom. He could figure out which direction the thoughts were coming from if he really concentrated.

He stopped this for a moment and then he saw a vision of himself and many other people locked in debate. The subject he could not hear for all of the people seemed to be speaking to him at once. Then he saw himself as he signaled all of them to be silent. Then one of the other men was asked to speak and he called Sylvester "Maris". He then suddenly realized that this was now his name. He stopped the vision and thought to himself for a moment. He then heard Adsideo' s voice inside his thoughts.

"You have now become a great leader of men Sylvester. You are now called Maris leader of the Ural people. You will lead them to great things. Remember your real name can only be spoken by one of us eight remaining Templars. Keep us secret and never discuss your real name with anyone." Then Adsideo' s voice was gone.

He jumped to his feet and ran to the balcony that adjoined his room. He looked over the railing and saw that there was a river running right in front of the balcony. There was a strip of trees between his balcony and the river but there was a river never the less. There was something familiar about this place. He did not recognize it at first. It would be some time later before it would come to him.

He then ran towards the door into the chamber and opened it. It opened into a great hall but it was not the same one he had entered into this room from.

What is going on, he thought to himself. This is very strange. He continued into the hall and found that there was only one other door opening into the hall. He entered through this doorway and found himself standing in a very large room that had a high ceiling that was a dome. The arched beams supporting the ceiling were painted gold. The inset in the center of the ceiling was the same mural of the three angels from the round window above God's throne.

All four of the rooms walls were opened to the outside by two sets of very tall doors that led to balconies that lay outside the door openings. The doors were open and the drapes were blowing with the wind. The sun was out and the sky appeared to be clear.

He stepped back out onto the balcony on his right side. Once outside he saw that the balcony was a very large one that encircled the room. At the end of the balcony farthest from him he saw that there was a great stairway that led from the ground below. In the center of the stairway was a guardhouse that was halfway from the ground and the main house. In the guardhouse there were no guards to be seen.

Where was he? He thought. Was he a guest here? Where were the others?

He could see down below that there were several houses and what appeared to be a small farm. There was a stable with a barn attached and several horses and lots of sheep and some cattle outside of them. There were chickens and ducks running around outside of the fences and running across the road he could see several children. From their dress it looked as if he was in the region of his homeland of Cheremis, but how could this be? Maybe during his sleep he had used his travel power without knowing it. Maybe he was still asleep. He was confused.

Sylvester ran back through the hall and into the bedchamber. There he found that the candle next to the bath was lit. He grabbed it and ran his hand over the flame until it burned him. He yelled and then he pulled his hand away from the fire and rubbed it on his leg trying to sooth the pain.

Well, this ruled out a dream. He thought to himself. He looked around to make sure one of the others was not watching him as if it was a cruel prank. He felt stupid.

He looked around the room and saw that it appeared the same as it had when he had gone to bed last night. He decided that maybe he would take a bath and surely this would awaken his senses to what had happened.

He walked over to the tub and dipped his hand into the water and found that it felt perfectly warm to his touch. He walked back to the door opening and shut the door. He picked up the door bolt from the corner of the room, where the door hinged from, and placed it over their cradle so as to lock the door shut.

He walked back over to the tub and undressed. As he stepped into the water he heard some men speaking.

They were close to the balcony. He stepped back out of the water and grabbed a tunic from the chair and walked out onto the balcony again. Down below he could see that there were two men heading up the grand stairway. They did not carry weapons and were dressed like farmers. They both wore wool head socks that covered half of their brow and had no brim. It was pointed and had a tassel on the end of it, which made it fold over to one side.

One of the men was tall and thin in his build and the other short and stocky in his.

The men came up the steps and when they stepped onto the balcony they saw Maris and stopped.

"So you have finally arrived master Maris," said one of the men. He spoke in a Uralic tongue, which had once been native to Sylvester as a child. This was a language that he could never forget. He thought of it a lot when he thought of his mother speaking to him.

"How do you know my name?" ask Sylvester.

"The man you sent to have us built this place for you told us all about you and your exile from the city of Jerusalem" answered one of the men.

"Where is this place Jerusalem at? Your man told us you could tell us once you arrived" said the other man.

"Maybe later" Sylvester answered cutting him off quickly and wondering to himself what it was exactly that they knew of him. Then Sylvester said, "May I ask who you two might be?"

"I am Drac," said the taller man of the two. "This is my nephew Cious" Cious bowed to Sylvester and his hat fell to the floor. Drac quickly bent over and picked up the hat and said "excuse my nephew, he is very clumsy sometimes. Please call on us if there is anything you need"

"Where is the nearest town or city" Sylvester asked them.

"Not to be to noisy but did you not come through the port city?" Drac asked while looking very puzzled at Sylvester.

"Drac, I meant other than that one!" said Sylvester, while trying to hide his own confusion. Where was this place? He thought to himself.

He looked out over the balcony and saw the river and the trees. He looked back to Drac and thought to himself that maybe he did not recognize this place.

"How long before you can have a few horses saddled and be ready to ride," Sylvester asked the two men.

"With in a very short time" answered Drac "Master Maris, dress yourself and we will bring the horses up here to the house when we are ready"

That is when Sylvester remembered he was still wrapped up in the white linen tunic.

"Then I shall be ready when you come back" Sylvester told them as he walked back inside the room.

Drac and Cious headed down the stairs and off to the stables.

Sylvester slid back into the tub and washed himself quickly. Once out of the tub he dried himself off.

Then he found a clean wardrobe of clothes lying on the bed. There was a very nice pair of black boots sitting next the bed.

Sylvester sat down on the bed and picked up one of the boots and tried it on. It was a perfect fit.

How could this be? He thought to himself. Who had come before him to prepare the villa? It had to be one of the three angels. Pridem? Nunc? Postorus? It had to be Postorus. Sylvester thought to himself. He was the future, was he not?

Sylvester removed the boot and then finished getting dressed.

Drac and Cious returned with the horses soon after. Once Sylvester heard them outside he walked out onto the balcony and over to the steps. Sylvester stopped and looked out over the estates grounds. The stairs and guardhouse faced the south. There was fencing setback an even distance on either side of the front and sides of the main house.

Beyond the fence to the right were the servant's house and the stables. Over to the left was a huge garden with several fountains and hedges surrounding all of the gardens.

To the left rear of the estate and for as far as could be seen were tree orchards of several species of fruits. These stood in front of a back drop of the mountains, which surrounded the countryside.

From where Sylvester stood he could not see to other section of property. What a nice place. He thought to himself. I think I could get used to this!

"Drac where is the nearest settlement. I wish to seek comradely from other locals!" Sylvester said as he began down the stairs.

"Why master Maris that would be Kazan, did you not come from there yesterday?" answered Drac.

"That is where we will go. How long will it take us to ride to this place?" said Sylvester.

"A day and a half through the valley. If the weather turns and we have to take the highway, two to two and a half days." Drac replied.

Sylvester knew then that he was near his homeland. This palace had either been built on the Kama or the Vyatka rivers. By the way the house sat and the river was along the bedchamber this river must be the Vyatka so that would mean that over the next hill is where the Kama, the Vyatka and the Volga Rivers all met together.

"Did you bring enough provisions for such a trip?" asked Sylvester.

"I brought enough food and grain for the trip but I will need to get another wineskin to make sure that you do not go thirsty, Master Maris" Drac replied.

"What kind of people inhabit this place "Kazan" asked Sylvester.

"Scythains, Turks, Huns, Cheremias, and Finns. Kazan is not a place a stranger to the country belongs. You should always watch yourself," replied Drac.

"I will try to remember that," said Sylvester "should we be on our way now?"

"After you, Master Maris" said Drac.

They all three mounted their horses and headed for the main gate passed the servants quarters and the stables. They were headed over the hill as the midday sun was on the rise.

And so began the first leader for this area to bring together a force of people known later as the Mari who would defend this area from being conquered by foreigners for many years and left an ethnicity that still remains there to this day.

Chapter Fifteen

(Dominic's story)

When Dominic awoke it was early in the morning and the sun was just peeking over the horizon.

He rose up from the bed and stepped onto the floor. As his feet touched the floor he looked down to see what his sense of touch had confirmed already. The floor was a dirt floor.

What was this he thought to himself? This had been a marble floor last night when he went to bed.

The others must have moved him outside the main house as a joke he thought to himself. Well it was early and they were probably still asleep so maybe he should play a joke of his own. He thought to himself.

He looked at the room and could tell he was in a thatched house with one window. This windows sill and jambs were framed with shall tree limbs. The roof was pitched and had thatch for the covering. There was a table and two chairs in the room and a washing bowl. This was the only other furnishing other than his bed. The bed was not the one he had fallen asleep in that was for sure. It was a wooden frame covered in straw and that was covered with a single blanket.

The weather outside was cool but not cold. It also seemed rather damp as well.

There was a single door leading from the room.

Dominic walked towards the door and opened it once he reached it.

Outside of the door was a small cramped room with a stone hearth and a rectangular table with eight chairs, three on either side and then one at each end.

Dominic walked out of the bedroom and into the main room. Once inside he could tell that this was all there was to this house.

On the other side of the table was the door leading outside. He walked in front of the hearth and in between the table towards the door. There was a good fire burning in the hearth and a kettle with a stew cooking in it. It smelt good. It made Dominic hungry. But this would have to wait.

He stepped to the door and pulled up the bolt and swung the door open. It was a heavy door he thought to himself for a thatched home.

He looked outside and saw that to the front of the house was a cobblestone walk leading to a small path that ran away from the house and into the trees.

Dominic stepped outside and walked a short distance out onto the walkway and stopped.

He turned back towards the small house and let out a sigh. All he could see around the area was trees. Huge oaks, elms, and hemlocks as far as one could see.

He could not see the mountain palace where he had slept last night! Surely they could not have carried him so far without him waking up. He looked around the tiny opening in the trees, where the house stood, for a moment while he tried to gather his senses.

"How can this be!" he said aloud. He was beginning to panic as he began to realize that there might be something more frightening to this scenario.

He turned back towards the house and marched back into the house to try and find an answer to this right away.

As he walked through the doorway he saw Adsideo sitting at the table.

"Adsideo how are you my friend" Dominic said.

"I am fine" Adsideo replied.

"Where are the others?" Dominic asked.

"It has begun" Adsideo said to him.

"What are you talking about" Dominic asked as he pulled a chair out and sat down across from Adsideo.

"The time has come for each of us to conduct our duties to mankind" Adsideo replied.

"I am glad I was able to get at least one nights sleep before the work began" Dominic said with a smile.

"Well, I see that you are rested and seem to be taking it well" Adsideo said to him "we are no longer at Sinai. We are in your native Island country. I will be leaving soon and it will be up to you to preach the word of God, teach equality, and show compassion to the uneducated men of this place. You must bring them together for our cause. You must build a nation and establish order"

"I guess this is your first time to travel to my homeland" Dominic said to Adsideo "this is a rough land of independent men. They seldom agree on anything"

"This will be your first task to accomplish. To get them to speak with each other. Get them speaking for a common cause and they will talk" Adsideo retorted.

"They will talk alright. Talk me into a hangman's noose" said Dominic.

"You will do fine" Adsideo said.

"Where will you be?" Dominic asked.

"I have a country of my own to nurture but if you need me to confer then just call and I will answer you," Adsideo told Dominic. Adsideo did not know if he should tell Dominic about his, Sylvester, and Arminius' s extra powers. He thought he had better wait on this subject for later.

"Where will I start?" Dominic asked.

"Here in this small house" Adsideo replied.

"Where is the nearest village?" asked Dominic.

"These are answers to questions that you shall seek on your own," Adsideo told him "you should practice you faith and rely on your magical skills as well. Practice these skills in secret for some may not understand your intentions.

They may see you as a threat since they are not as enlightened as you or I. I need to leave now. The others will be needing me soon" Adsideo said to him.

"Remember Dominic, you must be known by another name. A name has been chosen for you. It is from a local superstitious story about a man from this area. Your name is to be Myrddin Emrys. You are suspected to be the illegitimate son of a royal princess who was impregnated by either an angel or an incubus. Most think you are the latter of the two. Your grand father was a powerful and holy King by the name of Meurig AP Maredydd AP Rhain.

They believe that you were born evil but since your mother had you baptized in the name of our God at an early age that your evil side was erased but you kept your powers.

You were born at Caer-Fyrddin but moved here to this place and will name it Carmarthen, after your birthplace.

Here it is rumored that you practice white magic and you are a seer as well. People cannot find your home but, they will try. This place is protected by a magic that keeps others from entering unless you invite them to your home.

You must not reveal to anyone your true self. And remember the annual meetings which I will send further information for once the time gets closer" Adsideo said as he pushed his chair back and stood up and looked out of the window in the front of the house. How peaceful this land was he thought to himself? or was it?

"You are one of the lucky ones," said Adsideo "this is a rough and uncontrolled area, it is uncivilized but you will have plenty of time to spend by yourself to prepare for the task at hand"

"What you mean is this old man can be alone and thought to be crazy by his own standards," said Dominic.

"You used magic before, this will be your chance to practice the natural powers of the earth" said Adsideo.

"Even though I was permitted before, it can sometimes be like playing a dangerous game of tightrope between good and evil," Dominic said to him.

"Remember what God told us. How can we be wrong if we are setting the examples" Adsideo said.

"I do not think we are supposed to take that literal," Dominic said sharply, for he was angered by the way it seemed that Adsideo was using this term.

"I did not mean to offend you, Dominic. I merely wanted you to have confidence in this task and yourself." Said Adsideo.

"I will do fine, I know this. I must ask you to come and visit me every chance you get to. Just so I do not go mad," Dominic said.

"I will, I promise. You should seek some companionship from another source to fill in the times in between too." Adsideo told him as he walked over and put his hand on Dominic's shoulder.

"I must be leaving now. I will come to see you again soon. I must go to the others and help them understand what is happening with us now. I will pray for your success"

"May God go with you, Adsideo?" said Dominic.

"Myrddin, I wish you the same," answered Adsideo as he walked through the door.

Dominic stood from his chair to watch his friend as he let down the walkway but when he reached the window Adsideo was gone.

Dominic stood there for a moment puzzled. As he thought about what was just told to him he thought of the possibilities of what he may achieve as a magician in this land. It made him think of the stories of the magical men from far away places. the stories that as a child in this very place, he and other children were told about late at night by another sibling or a mischievous father.

He then turned and looked at the pot near the hearth where the smell of the stew was teasing his grumbling stomach.

He sat down at the chair that was near the hearth and took the lid off of the pot and the smell filled the room. It looked as good as it smelt.

He stood back up and walked over to a small cupboard and opened the doors. Inside the cupboard were bowls, plates, and goblets on the first two shelves and on the lowest shelf was a set of books. They were three in all and all had the same bindings. On their spines there was gold lettering that he was unable to recognize.

Dominic took one of the books from the outer side of the stack of books and sat it on the table. He then prepared a portion of the stew and filled the goblet with water. He sat himself, the food, the water and the book down at the table. He began to read from the book as he ate the meal.

The book and its drawings, sketches, and the strange lettering amazed him. He stared at a section of the second page of text and was suddenly able to see the words as if they were written in Hebrew text. Without even realizing it he was reading the incantation for the summoning of sprite fairies that began to buzz around his head. They were lit up on their bottoms and were quite a pest. He could hear small voices and laughter coming from them.

A couple of them were splashing the water around in his goblet. A few others were sampling the stew.

"What kind of trickery is this that you play on me?" he said as he picked up the bowl of stew. He put it up near his face and looked closely at the small beings. They were very tiny women about the size of ants. They wore small garments of clothing that was the source of the light that they emitted from their bodies. They also had very tiny sets of wings on their backs. These could not be seen except when they were very still.

"If you want something to eat then get your own from the pot. I am hungry enough that I might just eat you by mistake" Dominic said to the tiny creatures as he then began to put the bowl to his lips and started to drink the juice of the stew.

The fairies flew out of the bowl and away. One landed on his ear while the other sat on the tip of his nose.

He then began to hear the voice of the one near his ear as she told him that they could not fly near the hearth for the fear of burning up in the flames left them powerless to eat and if he would not mind would he please make a small portion for the fairies to share. She promised that other than this one little inconvenience they would go unnoticed for the rest of the night.

The one on his nose had walked up the bridge of his nose and was tugging on one of the hairs in his eyebrow. This was not real painful but his eye began to water.

"Alright little ones, but the first time I sense that you wish harm to me then I will smash you like any other insect" Dominic said to them all as he sat another bowl of stew down at the table for them. He could be heard for the remainder of the meal speaking to the fairies and reading the book.

And so began the first night for the old one who would later become the legendary white witch and scholar to the Kings as well as the commoner alike known to most as Merlin the magician and Myrddin of the wood.

He would have many, many other names as time moved on but we will get to this later.

Chapter Sixteen

(Laurence's story)

There was a warm breeze blowing through the window, which caused a shutter to creak. This had been what had awoken Laurence from his slumber.

The sun was coming through the window onto his face and made him feel sticky.

Laurence sat up in the middle of the floor. He had been laying on silken quilts and pillows. There was netting hanging from a frame, which was suspended by chain connected to the rooms ceiling. The netting draped every portion of his bedding.

As the netting fluttered in the breeze he looked through it as if it was not there.

It was the sounds from outside the window that had Laurence's attention. It sounded like a market place.

He stood up and discovered he was naked. He picked up a robe from the end of the bedding and dressed himself.

He walked to the window and looked out. There were people in the streets. He was in the city! How did he get here he wondered. He turned and looked around the room in which he stood. It was an average size room with plastered walls, which were a tannish-yellow color. There was the window in which he had stood in. There was a set of doors on the other side of the room and also on the adjacent wall as well. Two different sets of doors leading from the room. How strange he thought to himself. He only remembered a single door into the room he had gone to sleep in last night.

He walked to the closest set and opened them. It led into a hallway. He looked both ways but did not see anyone.

He shut the doors and walked to the opposite set of doors on the adjoining wall.

He opened this set and they opened onto a balcony. He walked out onto the balcony and stood there looking out over the city.

He knew this place. It was Tarsus of Cilicia. Tarsus was the name given this city long ago. This was also the name of the mountains and river that lie to the north of the city. The city lay at the end of this beautiful pass through the mountains, which was called "the Gates of Cilicia".

Much later in history Cleopatra and Mark Antony would meet for the first time here in 41 B.C. Also Saul of Tarsus would begin his life here as well. He later became would be known as the apostle Paul.

He was back to his birthplace. He had not seen this place since he had left the care of his old teacher Levian after being told that he could not be taught any more by the teacher and he had to leave and see the world for himself.

This had began Laurence's Journey, which eventually let him to become counselor to King Solomon.

He had been a good student of a very good teacher. He had learned philosophy, poetry, many of the written languages, art, and political debate. The latter was his passion.

Laurence thought of the many times he and his master had traveled to the market to observe the commoners as they bartered for items in the streets. Thus he was taught was how political aims and ambitions were bartered as well. "At least they should be" Lavian would say to his eager students.

He looked from the balcony over the buildings and could see the school that had been owned and operated by Levian. He thought to him self that he would get dressed and go to see who was there now. Surely Levian was elderly by now and could not possibly be teaching at such an age.

The building he was in was taller than most of the buildings in the city. He had a demanding view of the city and it's comings and goings through the city streets. To the left side of the balcony he could see the elevation of the land as it fell downward in grade and he thought he could make out the blue waters of the Mediterranean Sea. It had to be the horizon, he thought to himself. He knew that it must be a half of a day ride by horseback to Rhegma, the port and harbor for this city.

He looked back over to the right side of the balcony and looked at the busy streets. He could smell food being cooked and the smell of baking bread. He was hungry, he thought to himself.

Why? He had eaten heartily last night. He could not curb this appetite of his. His stomach was grumbling.

He thought he would find his clothes and get dressed and go down to the streets or somewhere in the house and eat.

He walked back into the room and found a wardrobe standing in the corner. He opened the doors and saw that there were several sets of clothes inside. He picked up a white linen loincloth, a red silken shirt, a leather apron, and a green sash. There was a set of sandals in the floor of the wardrobe.

Laurence picked up the clothes and shut the doors the wardrobe. He turned to go back towards the doorway when he heard Adsideo speak from behind him. It startled him at first, since he thought he was alone. He turned around and greeted his friend.

"Adsideo" he said "how did we travel so quickly to the place? Are we in a dream?" he asked as his thoughts took him to a sudden conclusion that maybe he was still sleeping at the Banquet hall chamber rooms.

"It is not a dream my friend" said Adsideo "it is time to fulfill your duties as a Templar. Set before you by God himself only a day before"

"I have not forgotten my duties but I may have lost my mind" Laurence said to Adsideo as he turned a shade of pale.

"You are fine, Laurence. You have been returned here to your place of birth as a kind or rebirth. It is here that you must use your political skills to influence the men of this area to love God and each other. You must use your education to bring together morals to the wretched men that you will meet coming as travelers to other far away places as well as the man on the streets. You will achieve great things and meet the pauper as well as the King" Adsideo told him as he walked toward the balcony. Adsideo walked out and looked over the edge.

"If you say so," Laurence said in response "have you become clairvoyant all of a sudden"

"You might say that. Could we speak about that later though? There are more important issues to discuss at this time" Adsideo answered him.

"As long as you answer my first question. How did we get here so quickly and where are the others?" Laurence asked of Adsideo.

"You did add a second question but I will answer them both" Adsideo told him. "The others are in their respective birthplaces or there near. You have been brought here by the will of God. This will be the only time that you will be moved like this. From here onward you will have to travel like other humans"

"Why so suddenly? Why were we not allowed to prepare better? Laurence asked.

"I do not have an answer for that my friend. All I know is that the series has begun and I have been told to make sure that all of you understand and remember of duties that we must complete" Adsideo answered the best that he could.

"How will I contact you or the others?" Laurence asked as he walked over and found a stool in the corner by the door to the hall. He sat down because he was feeling as though the breath had been taken from his body suddenly.

"I will be in Tyre, it is not that far away. If you call for me in your thoughts I will be able to hear you. Arminius and Sylvester will also be able to hear you" Adsideo told him. He did not mean to let out this extra bit of information but it kind of came out and he did not think about it until it had happened. He had to work on this skill of keeping his mouth in sync with his mind he thought to himself.

"How are you able to hear my thoughts? Can you hear them now?" Laurence demanded to know this and stood from the stool.

"We can only hear your thoughts if you ask for us by name" Adsideo assured him.

"Why only the three of you? Why didn't God give me this talent?" Laurence asked.

"I am not sure but he told us it was because we were the ones who delivered the Ark to him.

Look Laurence, I could have been any or all of us. But the fact is it was only the three of us. Do not make this out to be something it is not, besides it is quite annoying at times"

"Why do you say that?" Laurence asked.

"Well, I might as well tell you since I started this. We can also hear the wicked plans of the entire world as well as the sorrowful cries from the desperate and impoverished. It is hard to get used to listen them and remain clear in thought or speech"

"What can you do for them? How are you able to know how to find them?" Laurence asked as he walked back over and began to sit back down on the stool.

"It does not matter now. This does not burden you. Lets talk about what your new name will be. You shall have to get used to it quickly"

"I cannot chose?" Laurence asked, "Do you mind if I get dressed. I have a great hunger. Will you go and eat with me?"

"I suppose I could use a bit to eat" Adsideo answered.

"The food is very good here in Tarsus" Laurence told Adsideo as he completed dressing himself. He motioned for Adsideo to exit the door to the hallway.

As they stepped into the hallway a young girl of about fifteen or sixteen passed by who carried a clean rug to one of the rooms off of this hall. Laurence turned back to look at the girl and she at him as she turned to her left. She opened one of the many doors and exited from the hall.

"Where did she come from?" Laurence asked of Adsideo.

"You will learn that Hakan has many servants for his home" Adsideo answered him.

"Who is Hakan?" Laurence asked Adsideo as they reached the spiraling staircase that lead down through the round towers at either end of the halls. Laurence took the lead and they began down the stairs.

"That is who owns this grand palace. He is the master of the written tongue, he is the fair and disciplined one, he knows no spite or anger for he is a judge of men and holds the ear of the King" Adsideo answered him.

"Will we meet him later? I really am hungry and need to find something to eat" Laurence said.

"There will most defiantly be food prepared for him. I am sure you will not be hungry much longer" Adsideo told him as they reached the bottom of the stairs and walked though the arched opening which turned them out into the grandest of all the rooms that Adsideo or Laurence either one had seen to date.

One thing for sure was that Laurence followed his nose through this room and into the next hall, which lead to the dining room. As they walked though that room Laurence did take time to look over the wall decorations and the many balconies that surrounded the circular atriums different floor levels. He then realized how tall this palace was from the ground level.

They entered the dining room and found there to be many people sitting at the long tables.

"Lets us have a seat at the last table over there" Adsideo said to Laurence as he pointed across the room. They walked over to the specified table and were seated by a couple of young servants. The table setting was very nice. There were bouquets of flowers and dishes of food set out for all to eat. At each seat there was a plate and cup to use in dining.

"Will we get to meet Hakan soon? He sure has a nice palace," asked Laurence as the servants walked away.

"That would be possible if the plates were mirrors," Adsideo said with a smile. "You are to be known as Hakan to these people. You are the master of this house and will be very well known to all sooner than you will be able to fully understand unless you listen. Your knowledge of the truth is widely known to these people. You must follow along with their demands for your skills. It will be quite demanding at times," Adsideo told him, as he looked Laurence in the eye.

Laurence had stopped his eating and stared at Adsideo. He did not know what to say. He looked as if he had the air removed from his body again.

"Are you listening to me?" Adsideo said to Laurence.

"Yes, I am but I thought I would gain some rest after the ordeal with the Ark" Laurence said to him in reply" I am getting old you know"

"You shall if you organize your time as a servant to the people. But you must do as God willed and serve the people. Oh, and another thing, you are not getting older" Adsideo said to him "you must not forget that the lives of all will eventually rely on how we are able to manage their love and respect for each others perspectives"

"I understand and I will obey" Laurence said as he resumed his meal even though he was not as hungry as he had been when they sat down.

"Remember our yearly meet that must be attended by all eight Templars. We will notify you of its place before hand. You shall be responsible for you travel and it must be planned for at all expense" Adsideo informed him.

"Where are we to meet this year?" Laurence asked.

"It has not been set as of now but it will be soon," Adsideo answered.

"After your meal you are expected in the judgment room where you will be asked to judge the accused. Remember to be fair hearted but firm. You must try to restore the morals to a region that lives on the edge of momentary disaster at all times. Be strong brother" Adsideo told him as he stood from the chair and looked Laurence once more in the eye.

"Where are you headed to now?" Laurence asked as he looked up from the plate of food that he had been picking at.

"I must be leaving now. You will be fine. Remember to call upon me at any time"

Adsideo walked away from the table.

"Wait a moment I have more questions" Laurence asked of Adsideo.

"You shall have an attendant and advisor to help you with this" it was then that Abi walked over to the table. He had been standing near the servant's door to the kitchen area unnoticed.

He was an elder gentleman who stood over two cubits tall and was white haired.

"It is good to see you this morning, Master Hakan" Abi said to Laurence.

"Will you have a seat and eat with me," Laurence said to him as they greeted each other.

Laurence looked back to Adsideo to see that his friend was no longer there.

Laurence and Abi began to speak as Laurence began to ask about the schedule for the day. Abi told him of the accused and the background of each case. This intrigued Laurence and he regained his hunger as he resumed his eating.

And so began the leadership of Hakan who lead these people for many years and under many names at many different times. Laurence would leave Tarsus after a Lifetime and not return for several more Lifetimes. Upon each return he reorganized and established morals in the weak and wicked. His influences were recorded in many of the not to distant regions from Tarsus so he did not have to work extremely hard at this task.

He was later known under the name's of Sennacherib of Assyria, Homer of Smyrna, Xenocrates of Aphrodisias, and later even as Julian of Nicomedia. And of course as Saul of Tarsus. He was a bodyguard to the Christ child, Jesus of Nazareth, and soon after that he was know as the apostle Paul.

Chapter Seventeen

(Arminius'story)

Arminius sat up straight on the bench. He had been asleep at the table. The room was full of people. There was people making noise and talking. This did not make him feel well since he had a headache from the wine they had drank last night.

Where did these people come from? Arminius thought to himself. He looked around for the other Templars but did not see them. As he did so, he noticed that he was not in the banquet room any longer.

He saw that there were two doors from this room and one window. He stood up as he was going to find another room. He was going to find the others. He noticed the other men were dressed in warm furs and many different types of armor. The women were in many layered robes. These were very colorful and seemed well matched. How strange for the People of Sinai to dress this way Arminius thought to himself as he headed for one of the doors. He walked past the many other tables and right as he reached the door he saw Adsideo outside the window. Adsideo was standing in snow! What kind of Illusion was this?

Adsideo was wrapped in a robe made of a white bears fur. It blew in the wind loosely around the lower part of his legs. Judging from this the winds must be strong. Arminius thought to himself.

Arminius stood there for a moment staring at Adsideo.

Adsideo apparently saw Arminius and was motioning for him to come outside. Then Adsideo turned around, walked away and disappeared into the trees.

189

Arminius started out the door before he realized it he was outside and he had not obtained warmer clothing. He shut the door and found one of the servants and asked where he could find warmer clothing. The servant asked him to wait for a moment and she would return.

The servant returned and asked that he pay first and she would then bring the clothes for him and furnish a place of dressing.

"I do not have a great deal of time," Arminius said to her as he turned back to the door.

"You will not survive dressed like that" he heard her say as he shut the door behind him.

The wind was indeed blowing strong and sent a chill down his spine. Arminius treaded forward in the snow towards the tree line. As he entered the path he saw that there was a village over the crest of a small incline. There could be seen many lighted windows.

Arminius continued down the path where he soon found himself in between the many homes. He saw no indication that Adsideo was in one of the houses so he continued pass all of them until he found himself outside of the village.

The pathway had now turned into a road. Further on it made a fork. He looked right and then left again.

When he heard Adsideo tell him in his ever so reassuring voice to go to his left on the road.

He was cold and did not have a clear conscience. He wondered if that is what made him hear this. Then he heard it again but this time there was a vision flashed into his thoughts of Adsideo sitting in front of a hearth with a strong and warm fire burning in it.

Arminius quickly turned to his left and started down the road. He could hear Adsideo telling him every step of the way including warnings of deep wet spots in the snow. This finally led him to a clearing in the wooded area right off of the road.

There was a nicely built cut stone home with a wood shingled roof on it. This was stronger than the thatched homes he passed in the village. He knew Adsideo sat inside at the hearth and could not wait to get inside. He walked up to the massive front door and found it to be locked.

He knocked and could hear in his mind as Adsideo giggled about having locked his friend outside and knowing that he was cold.

"Very funny" Arminius said to him as the door opened. "I could get a cold from this and be sick you know"

"I do not think you have to worry about a cold," Adsideo said to his friend as he walked past him.

"Oh, this is what I need is some warmth and some explanation on where in the hell are we?" Arminius asked while taking his wet shirt off and laying it near the fire.

"I thought you would recognize this place?" Adsideo said to him "why I once remember you telling me you could sail a ship here even if the world was cast in eternal darkness"

"Oh, and nice of you to use the mind tricks on me before I have learned to use it" Arminius said to Adsideo.

"Do not worry it will come in time" Adsideo answered him as he walked over and sat near his friend.

"I need some warmer clothes," Arminius said as he began to take off his boots.

"There are plenty of clothes for you to wear in the next room," Adsideo told him as he became comfortable in the chair he had pulled closer to the fire.

"This mind trick is it related to the whispering I keep hearing?" Arminus asked.

"Mine came on like a roar" Adsideo said to him "it took some time to learn to quite it down in my thoughts"

"Maybe it is not as strong with me," Arminius said as he stood back up and walked toward the only interior door that there was and went into the next room.

"Where are the others and where are we at?" Arminius raised his voice so that his friend could here him from the other room.

"The others are in their birthplaces just like you are and soon I will be able to return to mine" Adsideo said to him from the other room.

"How did this happen?" Arminius asked, "How did we get here so quickly"

"By the will of God and the beginning of our duties" Adsideo told him.

"Then I do not have to stay here, I mean my family did live in one place but they were known to go on some what of a holiday ever now and then" Arminius said to him as he found a nice pair of leather pants and a matching shirt.

"I would not call pillaging every place they think would fill there pockets or fulfill their sexual needs for the moment, a holiday," Adsideo said to him in reply.

"Well I do not think I will win the hearts of my countrymen by staying at home" Arminius told him.

"You will abide by the code like the rest of us shall!" Adsideo confirmed this statement by hammering his fist down on the arm of the chair he was sitting in.

"I cannot voyage away from here at all?" Arminius asked Adsideo as he walked back in to the main room to see Adsideo eye to eye.

"You will be able to go where you will but you cannot expect men to listen to you tell them they should not kill each other the whole time that you are pillaging village after village. They must learn to travel as ambassadors not villains!" Adsideo said firmly "and just wait until you try the travel power. This can be quite confusing if you start to wonder in your mind of a another place while on the way to another. If you are not careful you will end up in the wrong place at the wrong time"

"Alright I understand now. There has not been this kind of outlook in my homeland in decades. It will be a time of renaissance," Arminius said.

"You must teach love and fair judgment," Adsideo said to him in a quieter more passive voice.

"Judgment by the people" Arminius said as he went back to the other room to complete dressing.

"Maybe it will catch on over time. That is as long as we do not give up on men's desires and help make them their possessions. You know, help their dreams become realities. It may be harder for some of us than on others but if you need help just ask for it" Adsideo said to him.

Arminius suddenly heard Adsideo say in his mind the name "*Alaric*". What did this mean he thought to himself only then to hear Adsideo say, "*this is your name for this generation*"?

"What do you mean this generation?" Arminius asked from the next room.

"You will learn the rest at the annual meetings," Adsideo said to him as he stoked the fire at the hearth.

"Alaric? I kind of like this name" Arminius said to him "it means ruler of all"

"That is right. So from this point forward you will be called Alaric and only the other Templars are to know your name" Adsideo told him.

"Tell me, Adsideo what is your new name to be?" Alaric asked him.

"Zaaru-Hayan" Adsideo told him "but for now and to you I will always be Adsideo. Like you will always be Arminius but to all others you are Alaric and after that you will be someone new with each passing generation."

"And you Zaaru-Hayan" Arminius said to him in retort with a smile. Arminius completed his dressing and saw in the corner of the room he was in, which was the bedchamber, that there was a door leading to another room.

193

He opened this door and saw that there was a stair leading straight down to a basement room.

"Save that for later my friend, come back and speak with me for I have to leave soon" Arminius heard Adsideo say to him through the mind trick.

Arminius shut the door to the basement and walked back to the main room and joined Adsideo.

"Why must you go so soon, I have just now dressed and you are leaving?" Arminius said to him as he walked into the room. Arminius then walked over to the wall adjacent to the hearth and pulled down a breastplate and helmet that was hanging on the wall. On either side of this were two broadswords and maces.

"My advice to you is to use this as your home. Do not allow anyone to know of this place. You must travel to the place of local politics and spread your words to the others of your kind. Go to a place that will be known as Tallin"

"I know of this place. I was told of it by my father and uncles long ago" Arminius said. "It is a great place of commerce and many ships harbor there during the long winter months," Arminius said to him.

"Go there and be aware of your duties. Make sure that all is kept secret. No one should ever learn of your real name so keep it silent at all times. I will be in touch with you as well as the others. Also be warned that should any of the other seven ever need you they can call for you by name and you will hear them" Adsideo told him "you shall always help them in anyway needed by the Templar code. Do not forget the travel trick and the abilities to travel backwards and forwards through time"

"How do I use this power?" Arminius asked.

"The only way I can explain it to you would be to tell you that as long as you have the will then it will take you that way" Adsideo said to him as he stood up walked to Arminius "keep a clear mind and a fair heart. Do not only live by the sword but, Live for the people" Adsideo then walked to the entry door and took the bear skin robe down from the peg it was hanging from and put it on over the mail shirt he was wearing. He then turned to Arminius and said to him. "Bring your people out of the woods and keep them civil while on the seas. Bring your thoughts to the table at the annual meetings, I will speak to you again soon" he then opened the heavy door and left the room.

"*Goodbye old friend*" Arminius said to Adsideo, using the mind trick. Adsideo answered back by telling him it would never be goodbye, only goodbye for now.

Arminius sat in front of the fire and thought of the days to come. He soon found that if he wondered about a place or a person long enough he could see them. He was not sure if he was witnessing the present or the future. He could also sense a great change in the way people thought.

He stood up went into the next room and opened the door to the basement and walked down the stairs.

And so began the history behind such legends of one man of many names. He liked to be known as Aegir, the Son of the sea. He was frequently seen in the fog and late in the night sailing his ship though the Baltic Sea and into the Gulf of Finland as if a reminder of his fellow men lost at sea.

Chapter Eighteen

(Democritus story)

Democritus awoke and quickly raised up from the bed he was laying in. He could here gulls and the sound of the sea. He knew it was the sea for the air was unforgettably damp and salty.

He must get up and find the others, he thought to himself.

He stood up from the bed and noticed that the room he was in was not the one he had fallen asleep in. this room did not have the stone walls which he had seen before falling asleep last night. This room was plaster walls with mosaic's of women and animals over the bed, an army in battle on the wall that held the door leaving this room. There were many palaces and various farms and estates painted on the other two walls.

Democritus heard the street noise, sounds like horse drawn carts, people yelling to each other, and various animal noises. He walked over to one of the two windows that were set side by side of each other and looked out into the streets.

He did not believe it but he was in Sestus, City of Thrace. How could this be? It had to be a dream he had not woken from. He could smell food being cooked over open fires and in ovens. People were everywhere. He could see the straits of Marmorn from here as well. The straight lead from the eastern world to the western world. He had been to the eastern countries along time ago. He had forgotten about these voyages all most entirely since he had been in service of King Solomon.

The ships could only pass one at a time due to the narrow straight and it also benefited the harbormaster as well. For Sestus had always had a heavy tax on the foreigners for as long as he had been alive. This also would become the downfall of Sestus in a later time.

How did he get here so quickly? He would go and find the others. He walked over to the closet he found in the southwest corner of the room and took out the clothes he found there.

He put on the clean loincloth and put on the green linen exomis (tunic), which he put on. He found a belt and put that on as well. There was a breastplate on the wall on the far side of the room past the windows. He took it from the wall and put it on. He found there to be a pair of Trojan sailors sandals next to the bed and he put those on too. They fit perfectly. The strangest thing to. When he put the right one on first, he saw that the impressions left by the wearer had the same impression as Democritus's own foot.

He heard someone speaking in the hall. He stood up and went to the door that led into this room and stood there for a moment listening. He could here the voices and they were both women. He opened the door very quickly and saw two women standing to the left of the door.

"May I ask which place I am staying in? Democritus asked. The two women looked at him with glazed over eyes and began to giggle. They looked back at each other as they did this and then began to half run and half walk away from him. He yelled to them "hey come back. I just want to know where I am at." Democritus said to them.

As he spoke these words he saw that there was a man that had come from one of the rooms from across the hall. he walked past the girls and towards Democritus.

"They do not understand what you say to them," said the man "they do not understand this language"

"Who are you and whose home am I in?" Democritus asked the man.

197

"Surly you jest master" the man replied, "maybe it was the journey from the frontier. Maybe you still have a fever..."

The man continued to speak until Democritus interrupted him and said, "Where are the men I can here with?"

"Why you were brought back here by your soldiers who found you. They said that they found you lying in your field tent delirious from fever. We had all but given up hope that you survived the campaign, master"

"Who are you and what are you talking about?" Democritus said to the man and then he demanded an answer.

"Master, it is I, Therapon, you do not remember me? I raised you when you were but a boy. Your father granted me with the charge along time ago. But it has not been that long since you left for battle. Have you lost all of your Witt?"

"Where are my friends?" Democritus asked again.

"I told you I do not know what you are speaking about" Therapon began to look away wards the other end of the hall as he repeated again "the soldiers brought you back to us"

"Alright, alright" Democritus said to Therapon "I did not mean to up set you. Maybe it is the fever but I do remember you old friend" Democritus told him this but did not mean it. He had not the faintest idea or whose house he was in and certainly did not recognize this man. He thought he had better play along with the old man until he found the others.

"Can I have food? I am very hungry" Democritus asked Therapon.

"Why of course, master. Right away" Therapon said to him as he whisked away down the hall. Democritus could hear Threapon yelling down the hall as he told one of the other servants to get the master of the house some food.

Master of the house? Democritus said to himself what was going on?

He turned around and went to shut the door when he saw something out of the corner of his eye! He ran towards the bed to grab his short sword when he heard Adsideo speak to him.

"Democritus, calm yourself. It is your old friend Adsideo"

Democritus turned around back towards the door and then back toward the windows. There was no one there. Had he gone mad he thought to himself?

"Where are you?" Democritus asked and the said "I cannot see you"

"I am not with you I am in another place but I can still hear you" Adsideo told him.

"I will not fall for this trickery! I know this is a trick! Maybe you are Bellabezzer himself!" Democritius said as he walked towards the window. He must kill this demon! This possessor of men's souls! He thought to himself. He would jump out of the window and kill himself and the demon. God would understand.

"No! Democritius. Do not do it! It is truly I. Adsideo. You cannot die remember! I do not have time to wait for you to heal either. Just Wait there for a few minutes and I will join you" Adsideo told him. Adsideo was nervous about forcing the time travel but did it at will. Soon he was at the palace wall and entered its gates from the northwest end of Sestus'es Main Street.

"I am at the gate. Bid your servants to let me in" Adsideo told Democritus through the mind trick.

Democritus thought this to be another trick so he would not leave his room.

Adsideo reached the entry door. He asked the sentry to allow his passage. He did not have any resistance since He used the mind trick on the sentry as well. Making him open the gate by suggestion alone.

Adsideo knew where to find Democritus but he did not know how to get there. He used the mind trick to gain this information as well and was soon standing in the hall outside of Democritus's bedchamber.

Adsideo knocked at the door. Democritus came to the door and opened it slightly enough to peep out. Once he saw Adsideo he was still weary about letting him in but did so with sword in hand.

"You can put the sword down! It is me," Adsideo said.

Democritus walked over and touched Adsideo as if he were in a dream or as if he were a ghost.

"Relax, it is I, in the flesh in blood" Adsideo repeated to him.

"Where were you? How did you speak into my mind like it was my ear?" Democritus asked.

"I have a mind trick that I will be able to speak to you if called upon. This time I called upon you" Adsideo answered him as he walked over to the window and began to look over the city.

"How did you get this power? Have you always had this power?" Democritus asked him as he was still dumbfounded by the events.

"Some of us were granted this power yesterday" Adsideo answered him "but it is not to be abused. It will be used to communicate among the Templars and also to hear the wretched and the deceived."

"I am sorry that I doubted it was you but after all we have been though in the passed few months I do not know what to believe or not believe any longer in what I see before me," Democritus said to Adsideo while his voice lowered to a whisper.

"You do not have to whisper, we are in your home. The servants will not repeat anything you say in your home" Adsideo told him "just beware of the potential spy. Keep your secrets with us and us alone. Be wary of quickly obtained friends in this hostile city of the Thracians.

You must try to bring some order to the region. Make sure that more cities are built, and there will be many to come. Make them get along and try to minimize the war and killing. Make them understand how to debate each other until resolutions are drawn."

"If this place is anything like it was when I was growing up, this will be very difficult to achieve" Democritus said to him, their conversation was suddenly cut off by the return of Therapon and several other servants. They brought food and fresh water for the washbasin, which sat near the entry door to the room.

"Master I did not know you had company?" Therapon said. All of the servants were busily preparing the table that was against the wall and centered in between the windows. "We shall have to bring more food for your friend"

Therapon told several of the servants to go down into the kitchen and bring more food for Adsideo.

"Therapon, this is my dearest friend. We fought together against many an army. I have been away to a far away land, which has taught me good things and good morals by which people should live. I would like for you to understand that there are to be changes around this house and for the people"

"Yes master. I will tell the entire house. Right away" Therapon told him as he began to bow away from Democritus.

Then Democritus told him to stand still for he was not finished speaking to him.

"Why of course Master. I shall learn" Therapon asked in forgiveness.

"My friend here will be respected as I am in this house!" Democritus said to them all. "Therapon, keep my orders in this house. I shall make my announcements to the public myself. If there is anyone that cannot be trusted then send them away from here!"

"I shall see to it. Right away master" Therapon said as he began to muster the other servants away. Therapon and the servants left the room.

Democritus walked over to the table and sat down. He asked that Adsideo join him.

"I shall eat a little. We must talk about your future" Adsideo told him as he sat down and joined Democritus at the table.

"Have you become a fortune teller or a seer, Adsideo?" Democritus asked with a smile. He prepared a second plate of the food and sat it in front of Adsideo.

"You will learn that I do know a little about something," Adsideo told Democritus "we must talk about your duties to your kind and the responsibilities that you will have to fulfill. You are one of the few Templars that will be allowed to keep your birth name. You will influence a great deal of people in the future and God wills that your name be associated with this from now on. You will enjoy your duties more than any of us. You will lay an egg of knowledge for all mankind that will be born for all to use. You must keep these ideas in the nest for now but keep your thoughts warm and they will one day hatch into the greatest foundation for civilized man and government. Many will be blind and you have to make them see. You will meet the sick and you shall heal them. You are to be the father and grandfather for the rest of the free world for all time. It is upon your accomplishments that will be echoed around the world for all to hear!" Adsideo told him. He then began to eat the meal as he awaited the response from Democritus.

"I do not think popularity is one of the things I should try to accomplish if I am trying to be secretive in our endeavors" Democritus state to Adsideo "I do not understand how to do this without being discovered by all that will listen to me. What will be the foundation for my claims"?

"Faith in God and mankind will be that foundation you seek. You shall find a way. I will help you" Adsideo told him in retort as he washed his food down with a cup of the wine. "Things will be done right by you Democritus"

"This sounds like demons work to me" Democritus said to him "I do not feel right about deceiving men into a course of action that may not be corrected in the event of an altercation or mistake"

"Remember what we were told by God. How can it be wrong if we are the ones making the rules? Do not worry so much my friend. You shall do fine in your tasks. I will personally see to it." Adsideo reassured him as he continued to eat.

"You are hungrier than you thought huh," Democritus said to Adsideo to change the subject.

"I just ate with Laurence a little while ago. I did not think I would be this hungry but this meal is very good" Adsideo told him as he drank from the cup again.

"You see the others? Are they as well as I am? I want to see the others. Take me to them" Democritus asked of Adsideo.

"Slow down my friend, it is not that easy and besides it is not time. We will have the annual meetings. You shall see them then" Adsideo told him.

"Tell me where they are at. I will seek them on my own" Democritus said to him.

"You may see Arminius and Sylvester as you see me here now. For only they have the powers I do. They can speak with their minds and travel at will. If you would rather see them then it will be done. We are able to deny any requests if we are busy though," Adsideo told him as he began to eat from the plate again.

"Who do the people of this house think I am?" Democritus asked.

"You are the son of a brave and valiant field General. You left for battle some years ago. You were most recently found on the banks of the river Danube almost in the enemy's hands at Buda.

Adsideo explained to him "though the army you command and the principals that you will teach. You will set the foundation for all of mankind. Others will not listen and set up domains for their own greed and not for the protection of the people but one thing they will see over and over is that no one will ever establish a free form of rule over the people like you will"

Democritus looked up from his plate and grabbed his cup. He took a drink of the water and washed down his last bite of food. As he sat the cup back down he looked Adsideo in the eye and said. "I will do as you ask but the first time I feel that I am misleading the people then I shall govern them on my own"

"Do not worry brother, I will honor your thoughts as if they were my own" Adsideo assured him.

"I must be leaving soon. There are a couple of the others who will need my help soon" Adsideo told him as he wiped his face. Do you mind if I wash up before I leave?"

"Help your self. My house is your house Adsideo!" Democritus answered him.

Adsideo stood up and walked over to the washbasin and washed his hands then his face. He then dried off his face and walked back over to the table. The whole time Democritus watched him as if from afar.

"Will you come back soon?" Democritus asked him as he himself stood to bid his friend goodbye"

"I will. You should go down to your reception room and see your field commanders for they are preparing a launch against your nemesis very soon. You are expected to join them in this task. You should weight the future very carefully Democritus" Adsideo told him as the shook hands and exchanged embraces. "Remember you are the one. Use your decisions carefully and select your friends the same way. I will inform you of the place for the annual meeting as soon as we decide where to have the first one. I will be speaking to you soon"

"How will I know that you're the one speaking to me? That makes me very nervous when you do that" Democritus said to him.

"I will say the words Democritus, it is your best friend. Then I will speak to you. Will that do?" Adsideo told him as he walked over and open the door leading to the hall.

"That will be our code then for the mind trick anyway," Democritus said as he smiled and bid his companion goodbye.

Adsideo walked out into the hall and began to shut the door when Democritus told him he would see him to the gates but Adsideo told him there was no need and would prefer to see himself out.

When Democritus insisted and he turned around to get his weaponry. When he picked up the sword and placed into his belt he heard Therapon begin to speak. "Master hear is the food for your friend" Therapon said, "Oh, I did not know that he left"

Adsideo was nowhere to be seen. He had left in an instant! How could this be?" Democritus thought to himself.

"Yes, he is gone. I sent him on a very important mission" Democritus said to Therapon "he is to travel ahead of me and the troops"

Therapon thought this to be very strange since there was only one exit that he knew of from the hallway and that was down the stairs. Therapon had been standing at the bottom of the stairs awaiting the servants to bring the food for their master and he had not seen Adsideo leave.

He had been living here a very, very, long time and had never seen anyone leave this house in another manner.

"Do not worry about my friend. He will return soon with the news I require," Democritus said to him.

"Now take me to my reception room and have my men meet with me there" Democritus said to Therapon.

"But Master, Lycios has left for the docks and is preparing an attack on the Persians" Therapon said to him in return.

"Then send for him! Now! Democritus yelled at him as he raised his arm and pointed towards the door.

Therapon quickly left the room and went down the staircase quickly. He found the closest foot soldier and had a messenger send for Lycios.

Democritus adjusted his armor and left the bedchamber. He proceeded down the hall until he found the staircase that led up or down. Democritus went down the stairs. Once he reached the bottom of the stairs he found himself in the main foyer. From there he walked back to the right hand side and then entered a large room.

There were people standing about as well as many others filling all of the chairs and benches that lined the walls.

Each and every one of them either changed the subject that they were speaking about, to the subject of Democritus or they stopped talking all together as he passed by them.

The next room he entered was like an entire building of its on. It had the highest ceiling that he had ever seen.

There were balconies on the walls that stepped from the floors above. Along each floor level, the balcony railing was made into a planter box where fern, vines, and many species of flowers where growing from.

Democritus saw that there were many people on each of the floor levels including the ground level, which he stood.

There were wall sconces that held very large brass rings through them. Through the rings, hung woven linen draping of many colors. These linens ran through one ring to the next at each point the linen draped to the floor and back up again until it encircled the entire room. From each of the wall sconces flames rose and died back-and then only to rise again. This caused the room to be dim in places.

The floor had been made of terrazzo since he had left the stairs leading from his bedchamber, and was a garnet color through out except in this room. There was a large circle bordered by a square design. This was made entirely of black granite. The circle design was made of a blood red terrazzo. Inside of the circle was the garnet color except the symbol, which was also inlayed terrazzo of various colors.

As soon as Democritus reached the symbol in the floor there was applause by the people in the room that startled him.

He was walking to the steps that led to the upper rooms. As he did, there were several Magi priest that were beginning to walk down the steps to meet him. Democritus would receive a load of information and teachings from these Magi. This would lead him to define his thoughts on management of men and the political systems of the old world. He would think of nothing else except how to refine these actions from now until his demise.

And so began the new life of Democritus. He was also know in his future as Alexander III of Pella, Caranus of Orestis, Thucydides of Athens, and Plato, Plotinus of Rome and many others though out time.

Chapter Nineteen

(Colin's story)

It was raining. The raindrops were large and made a large splat as they hit the stone facade outside of the window. Inside of the room there was a stirring below the blankets and once the corner of blanket was thrown back it revealed Colin's face. He stretched his arms up into the air and yawned as he sat up on the straw mattress in which he had slept on.

As he looked around the room he could not believe his eyes. He was in his Grandfathers room at Drakes Craig.

Colin knew this could not be! This could not be true. This was one of those illusions he had suffered from during the previous days. They had to be illusions right?

When Colin had left this isle the last time he had vowed that it would be the last time that he would see this place. There was nothing here for him. All of his family except his Grandfather had either despised or hated him or in his sisters case deceived him. This was only a place for bad memories.

He threw his legs over the edge of the bed and stood on the stone flooring. There was a bit of a breeze, which caused him to scramble to look for some clothes. Though he was not cold he could feel the breeze on his skin and this did not feel natural. He felt different somehow. Something about him was changed. But he could not figure it out right now.

He found some clothes in a chest at the end of the bed. He put on what amounted to a one cubit wide by three cubits long blanket with was hemmed at the sides that had small brass discs at four points across the chest and on each of them was one of the symbols for the elements.

This was also fastened with a wide leather belt, which was also lying in the trunk. Then he put on a sash over his shoulder and attached it with a buckle at the shoulder. He found Saorsa, his grandfather's broadsword and sheath setting up in the corner of the room. He remembered this sword from the days of his youth. He had a many a time snuck it away from his grandfather and played with it. He had loved to act as if he was a conquering warrior on some knight from a far away campaign.

He dreamed of leading a great army against an evil foe. He remembered the scolding he had gotten when his grandfather had awoken to find Colin in the courtyard of Drake's Craig hacking at one of the many apple trees. Needless to say Colin's chores were doubled for a while as well as his standing time on his feet. It had become difficult to sit for a couple of days afterwards. This was due to the thrashing he had received for putting a nick in the blade of Saorsa.

He walked over to it and picked it up. He unsheathed it and held it up to the light and allowed it to shimmer off of the blade until it bounced into his eyes. He saw the nick in the blade was still there. He then put back into the sheath and threw it over his shoulder as well. He then turned towards the door and walked into the hall and over to the stairway that lead to the main room.

He had played many a time as a child on these stairs before being run off by his sister or one of the nannies. Then in those days, as a child, he would run off into the estates large grounds.

His family the Pickens had inhabited this isle so long ago that none of the original stories held much truth since they had been told so many times over that they were mainly believed to be legends.

There were paintings and tapestries hang all along this stairway and leading down into the main chamber where all of the family business had been conducted when he was a child.

The room was dusty and unkempt. All of the furnishings were disrupted, toppled, or missing. There were spider webs all about the corners and the chandeliers. The steppes were also covered in dust and he left footprints on them as he walked down.

When he entered the main room he could see that there were bodies of dead men and women laying in the floor and hunched over the table as if struck down while they were eating.

They were dead long ago for there was barely the slight stench of decade bodies. They were merely bones wrapped in whatever clothing, which remained on them. He walked over to the far end of the table where his grandfather's body sat in the high back chair as if he was sleeping. Colin sat down on his knees and stared up at his grandfather's remains. His body almost gone but it appeared to Colin as if he had been smiling during his death.

Why would his Grandfather left his sword in the room above?

He always wore this wherever he went as long as Colin had ever been alive and living on this isle.

Colin walked at first and then began to run towards the main doors leading to the stone courtyard outside.

Once on the landing that sat above the stairs that lead to the courtyard. He stopped and saw the decayed plants and trees that used to fill the courtyard with the sweet fragrances of fruit and flowers. He just stood there wondering to himself about what might have happened here and what he had just seen. He began to feel the water swelling up in his eyes. He would not cry right now he told himself. He grabbed the stone trellis railing on the porch and heaved in the emotional pain as he tried to push this anger and sadness back inside. He then straightened his body and began down the stairs when he suddenly stopped halfway down and sat on the stairs. Saorsa clanked against the stone stairs and the shoulder strap hung against the neck forcing him to push it back behind his back. He sat there and cried for a moment. As he did this the memory of his father and brothers flashed into his mind. He stood up and began to run towards his father's estate, which was half a day's ride from Drakes Craig.

Colin ran until he reached the first tree line of the estate. He stopped and rested against a tree and just stared back at Drakes Craig. He did not know of any of the other clans that would have done this. He wondered if the territories had been invaded? Where were his brothers?

He would find out! He began his journey through the woods. The path though here had not changed since he was a young boy and probably longer than that. There were several species of oak, elm, and walnut trees through out the woods on the Isle of Skye.

As he walked along he looked at the pathway and it dawned on him that there were no horse tracks or any other animal tracks either. This was very strange indeed he thought to himself.

There was going to be more to this to be discovered than he would find out for quite sometime.

He slowed his pace to nothing more than a fast walk. This was because he soon began to remember how long of a journey it was from his father's estate from Drakes Craig.

He soon came upon a small cottage that was a shambles, and he could see that there was a fire in the hearth inside of the small one room house.

He walked up towards it and did not see anyone outside the premises. He walked up towards the door and yelled for anyone that might be inside. Suddenly the door opened up and there stood Adsideo.

"Adsideo, what kind of mind tricks are these that plague me? Why have I been brought back to this dreadful place?" Colin asked as he stood there and stared at Adsideo. His eyes again began to well up with the tears.

"This is the place of your birth. This is yours to claim once and for all time." Adsideo told him "come inside and let us talk for a while"

"I do not want talk!" Colin said to him "I want revenge for the death of my grandfather. Then I want to leave this nest of bad memories"

"No, what you really need right now is to sit and listen to what has happened here so you will be better informed as to how to react like a Templar" Adsideo said to him in a very aggressive manner which left Colin with no other option then to listen to him. He was shocked by this tone. He had not heard this for such a long time. He thought back to himself quickly that the last time he had heard Adsideo speak in such a tone. It was the last time that he was grilling them on the defense of Temple before the battle against Shishok.

"Colin come inside and listen to what I have to tell you. This will allow you to know who has done this to your grandfather.

They both stepped into the one room cottage and the door was drawn shut by the rope and counterweight that was attached to the door and then back into the corner of the room.

"Come and sit, I have some bramble wine we can have some of this while we talk." Adsideo told him. They both sat down and looking across from each other. Adsideo picked up the clay pitcher in which the bramble wine was in and poured them both a portion of it in the cups that sat on the wooden table. There was a small oil-burning lamp there as well. The cottage was scarcely furnished with little more than the table, chairs, and what appeared to be a bed frame covered in furs and hide of many kinds. They were stacked one over the other and there were leather pillows stuffed with feathers of birds laying on top of this bedding.

"Colin I must tell you some things that will upset you even further. You must promise me that you will not leave this room until you have heard all I have to say" Adsideo continued to speak to him "after you left this place as a boy. Your grandfather disowned your father due to the way he raised and treated you and your siblings. He loved you so much that he told your father that he would not be allowed back at Drakes Craig until he brought you back before him. Your grandfather would not see your father's face ever again from that day forward. He died never seeing any of his namesakes.

Your Father spent the remaining years searching the entire western world for you.

After the death of your father, which came, many years before the fate that befell your grandfather, your brothers decided that they would reclaim from your grandfather what they felt was rightly theirs. They lay a siege to Drakes Craig that lasted over a year. Your grandfather's forces held them until the last minute but did fall in the end. Every last one of them died in the defense of the castle. It was a very valiant and noble battle indeed.

Your grandfather was stuck down by a poison, which was induced by one of the cooks. Your brother, Chalmers threatened the cook. The cook frightened by the threat of not only death for himself but for his family as well. He was given the poison in which was put in your grandfather's last meal. That is why you found all of his court lying about like you did. After the meal was served the cook and his family were murdered any way by your brothers." Adsideo told him.

Colin took a drink of the Bramble wine and looked at Adsideo speechless. He did not know what to say. He looked about the room and then back to Adsideo and said, "how am I supposed to feel about this?" he asked Adsideo "there was no love for me here other than my grandfather"

"Your sister was very loving to you" Adsideo said as he put his cup down and looked at Colin.

"But in the end she left me to my grandfather while she too ran away" Colin answered him as tears began to stream down his face again.

"She was young and that was her way of coping with a problem," Adsideo told him "she has now returned to the island shire a widow. She thinks of you often. She misses you but believes that you are dead"

"And my brothers? Are they still here?" Colin asked.

"No, they are all either dead or gone from here in disgrace. The remaining surrounding clans of Picts saw to it that there would be no commerce between the Pickens and the remainder of the clans. They soon were driven out and the remaining died by the hand of their own brothers" Adsideo told him.

"Then there will be no revenge for my grandfathers death?" Colin said as he stood from the table and walked over to the one and only small window opening in the room. He looked out as he heard Adsideo tell him that he was to reclaim Drakes Craig and bring order to the clans. He was to visit with his sister for she would be able to support his claims to the other clans. Adsideo went on to tell him of the highlanders that were ever encroaching on the ancestral lands. He told him how the McLeod's and the MacDonald's of the highlanders were ever more and more, drawing plans to raise claims to the Pickens lands. Colin walked back to the table and sat down once again.

"Pour me another" Colin asked as he raised his cup to Adsideo who poured his cup full this time.

Colin raised the cup and drank it all down at once. Some of it leaked out of his mouth and ran down his chin.

"Colin you must listen to what I am telling you about bringing the clans together. You not only bring together the Picts and Scots but the Erie as well." Adsideo continued to tell him.

"I cannot be expected to do this thing! This has never even been thought of much less done," Colin said to Adsideo while downing the last cup of Bramble wine.

"That is why you will do it!" Adsideo told him in response "you will and you shall. Colin, there will be large and powerful forces that will wish to conquer this place. They will come from different shores to this isle and will take your women and children if you do not start to do something now. Before it is to late. We will all be counting on you" Adsideo told him this as he stood up from the chair and began towards the door. "Colin, my friend. I hope you have listened to me and you will remember your duties to God. The safety of these people is in your hands. Think with your head and not with your hands. Judge by your heart and not anger"

Adsideo opened the door and walked outside as he asked that Colin join him. Colin obeyed his captain. "Colin do not forget that all you know about the Templars and the siege at Jerusalem shall remain a secret. Do not ever forget this. No one should know. And remember that mankind is depending on us whether or not they know it. It is better that they do not know it. Make them believe that it is up to them and they might act a little more responsible"

"I will listen and do my best" Colin told him as they stopped to talk at the nearest tree off of the trail. "I do not see how I will get this done but I will do my best"

"Do not worry Colin, I can always be reached by thought. I will be there to help guide you if needed" Adsideo told his youthful young friend.

"Remember go to your sister and then at the next council of the clans speak to them and make them understand that you are here to reclaim your birthright and

215

then teach them what you have learned about God and the ways of miracles, but do not tell them of our pact. Also there you will find in the basement levels of Drakes Craig you will find a vast fortune that was amassed by your grandfather. No one ever knew of this except him and a few of his men that were paid handsomely to forget about it. One of them is still alive but living as an estate owner him self in the lands of the Brits. Use the wealth to restore Drakes Craig and bring back your grandfathers good name. That shall be your revenge"

"I hear what you are telling me I will heed your call for my duties" Coin answered him.

"Colin I must be going. I have to meet Maurice and then I will be in Tyre after that. If you need me call for me in your prayers and I will answer you as quickly as possible" Adsideo told him as he laid his hand on Colin's shoulder. He turned his younger friend to look him in the eye and said.

"Colin I will see you soon"

"Adsideo, where will I find my sister?" Colin asked him.

"On the northern edge of the woods, northwest of your fathers estates" Adsideo answered him "I will need to go now. I will see you soon. Do not forget the annual meeting, I will tell you where soon enough"

Adsideo began to walk down the pathway leading off to his father's estates.

Colin watched as his friend disappeared into the trees. Colin walked back towards Drakes Craig. He thought he had better go and see the treasure and at least find something worth trading for servants and horses. He would need to buy materials and labor to restore the castle, Drakes Craig. He could not wait to see his sister either.

Colin continued towards the castle as he walked down the pathway he looked back to see if he could see any sign of Adsideo though the trees. He could not.

Soon he reached the meadows surrounding the Craig and he could see it once again. How dreary it looked! He would have to fix this he thought to himself as he walked on towards it.

And so began the history of the Scots and very soon afterwards Colin also founded the Isle of Erie between his lives in the highlands.

Chapter Twenty

(Maurice's story)

Maurice woke up in a sweat. It was hot in the room in which he slept. There were sounds of people bartering with each other. He could hear this coming though the windows. Some were laughing and some seemed disgruntled. Maurice stood up and saw that he was in a sandstone and plaster home of some kind. He looked around and saw that there were three windows in this room and all of them were covered by curtains and filled by the sounds of the people outside. He walked over to one of the windows and looked out. He could see that he was near the port of this city. He looked around at the people out there and could see that they were Pelusiumites! How could this be? He walked back over to the bed area and saw the door that must lead out of here and walked over to it. He opened the door and walked into a rather large room. There was a sunken pit floor in it that was covered in hewn sandstone and laid in mortar. This was covered in pillows and rugs. Past the pit and along the right side of the room was a long table against the wall in which a window sat above the table. On the table were fresh vegetables and meats and several containers of different kinds. To the left of the table was a washbasin that had a trough leading to the out side. This trough emptied the washbasin into the garden that was outside of the window.

To the left side of the room were entry doors that led outside to more flourishing plants and flowers? There were cobble stone paths leading in various directions. On either side of the doorway there were large statues of one of the Kushite or Egyptian Gods. He did not like these being there. Where was he? This was not pleasing to him. There was some trick here he thought to himself.

He walked back around the room and admired the other carved stone animal figures and the wall carvings. All of which were Egyptian in design. He was in Pelusium but why all of these Egyptian art pieces? He was going to find the others and find out what was going on. Maybe this was one of Bellabezzer' s tricks. He walked out of the entry door and out into the gardens. There was the bright sun and birdsong. He saw that on this side of the house there was a great wall surrounding this garden and it blocked his view of the street as well as theirs from him. The paths were wide and meandered around various palms and other plants. There were two fountains that he could see through the shrubbery and plant life. They to were of Egyptian design.

He could make out the gates at the far end of one of the paths. At this gate there were two guardhouses one on either side of the gates. There were guards in them as well. Was he a prisoner? Had some adversary captured him during his sleep? Surely not from God's secret caverns.

He looked to see if there were any other houses on this property but could not see any. He decided that he had better walk around the house a little more to see if he could find any other sign of what had happen to him and the others. As he walked around the path that hugged the closest to the house he saw many benches and sitting areas that were beautifully landscaped around then. How peaceful this place was. He continued to walk around until he came to a discreet area of the home that had a detached room. This could not be seen until you walked past the opening in the floor that led to the subterranean stairway. There was no sign that there was a room below ground other than this opening to the stairway. Over the top of this sat one of the two fountains. This one had the figure of a falcon headed human image with its wings spread out as if it was going to wrap its wings around the next person to venture to close to him. Water was spraying from the falcon's beak, which was slightly open. On its head were the symbols of the serpent and the jackal.

Maurice looked into the opening to the stairs and saw that at the end of the steps was a red painted door. He walked down the stairs and grabbed the doorknob, which was gold and shaped like a snakes head and upper body section. He turned the knob to the left and the door swung open the same direction. There was a lighted hallway that had torches hanging in brackets along the wall. There must have been hundreds of them. The hall led slowly downward into the ground. He could not see the end of it in sight just row after row of torches.

Maurice continued down the hallway until he came to the first of the many doorways that lined this hallway. This one was on the right side of the hallway. He looked inside and saw that it was filled with the most intriguing furniture that he had ever seen in his life. All of it was from a culture, which he had never seen before. It looks like it was a cross between Pelusium and some other culture. All of this was made of gold or something that shined like gold. There were leopard skins covering almost all of it. Some of this was covered in color dyed linens. There were urns and wine vessels everywhere, there was a table or any kind of sitting device.

Maurice walked into the room and walked around the furnishings to see if he could recognize this strange culture that had made these items. He did not see anything that made him realize who had made it but he did like it, wherever it came from. He sat down on one of the sofas and laid back on it. It was very comfortable. He saw that on one of the tables next to the sofa there was a tray, which had some dates and a cup of wine on it. He started to drink from the cup when he suddenly thought of the others. What was he doing down here wasting his time when he needed to find the others as quickly as possible. What if they were in trouble somewhere? He thought back to when he first woke up. Was there anything in the room, which would show a sign of trouble?

Maybe he would go back to the house and see what was going on.

He stood back up from the sofa and began to walk towards the door when suddenly he tripped on something and fell to the ground.

This stunned him and came totally unexpected. It had caused him to hit his head on the floor.

Maurice quickly stood up and grabbed his head with his right hand. He rubbed a spot on his forehead, which had already begun to swell. He looked at his right hand and saw that he was bleeding from the wound on his head. It did not appear to be a bad wound for his hand did not have that much blood on it. He then took a small cloth from his battle apron and put it to the wound.

He was also a little dizzy and his eyes were watering. They did not focus well at first but it was getting better in the first few moments.

He stood there for a moment longer and as he looked toward the doorway he saw a flickering shadow on the hallway wall. He knew that it was someone or something tall. The shadow covered the far hallway wall from where he stood. He stared at the wall and watched in earnest as to see if this person or thing was coming toward him or away from him. He stared but did not see the shadow again. He then decided to investigate. His head was ringing with pain. He could not believe he had fallen so easily. He walked to the door opening and looked into the hallway. First to the right and then to the left. He saw nothing unusual that he had not seen when he first came down the ramp him self.

He looked back to his right for this is the way that he felt the shadow had been cast from. He slowly cleared the door opening as he headed into the hallway.

As he walked he felt as if someone was following him. He kept looking over his shoulder. But each time there was nothing to be seen. He was slowly moving along the hallway looking this way and then that way. He came up to the next doorway. This time it was on his left hand side. He hugged that side of the hallway as he crept closer to the door opening.

Maurice peeked around the corner of the door opening.

There in the middle of the room was a water fountain with a circular receiving pool below the image of a dolphin. The Dolphin was cast in polished gold. It seemed that it was meant to look as if the dolphin was either headed to the surface or caught in mid flight during a lunge above the water.

On the other side of the room was a stairway leading out of the room and to the surface level.

Maurice headed straight for the stairway and opened the door at the top of the stairs.

He walked through the door and found him self standing inside of a small shop. He walked over to the window and looked out. He could see the wall that surrounded the estate, which he had, woke up in this morning. He opened the door leading outside and stepped out onto the street. He stopped just short of a women walking right towards him as he entered the street from the shop. He looked back at the shop and saw that there was a red sign, which had a white dolphin jumping out of water painted on it.

Maurice remained there for a moment looking each way down the street.

"This is Pelusium alright!" he said out loud "there is Axius livery stables"

A man that was passing by him in the street saw Maurice talking to himself and stared at Maurice as if he had seen his first crazy man of his life. Maurice saw this and stared back and also growled at the man as he passed by.

Maurice did not think twice as he headed for the livery stable. He walked into its doors and looked for the first livery worker he could find. It was a man cleaning out one of the many stables.

"Where can I find the owner of the stables?" Maurice asked the man.

"I will go and get him and bring him here to you" the worker replied as he sat the pitchfork he had been using in the corner of the stall.

While Maurice waited he walked back to the livery stable doors and watched the people in the streets. He could see a glass merchant's shop where he was busy blowing glass in various shapes.

There was a food market on the farthest corner from the livery stable and women were busy looking at the green vegetables. He watched as men and animal drawn carts passed by him.

He remembered playing in these very streets while Axius and he were on their way to sail the terracotta boats that his mother had made them. And as always Axius would be in these memories.

Now he had a different agenda for Axius. Maurice knew that Axius was the only one who knew who he was and when he was leaving here the last time he was here in Pelusium. He did not know what he would do but he was going to take care of this little fact here and now he thought to him self as the memory of his sister's head stared back at him from in the well. Along with all of the other people in Arsinoe. He had made sure that the Egyptians had paid then, now it would be Axius's time to pay. This would end this painful topic for once and for all as far as Maurice was concerned.

"There he is" said the livery stable worker to a man he had brought back with him. It was not Axius that was for sure.

The man began to walk towards Maurice with a look of much needed explanation.

"I did not mean to take up your time. I asked the boy to bring me the owner of this establishment," Maurice said to the man before he reached Maurice.

"Then that would be me" the man said to him in reply "what would you need from me that the boy could not have taken care of?" the man asked.

"I did not mean to bother you. I needed to speak with my old friend Axius" Maurice said to him as he acted a little angry with the mans vocal tone towards Maurice.

"If you were really his good friend you would know that he has been dead for almost a whole harvest season. Blown away with the wind he was" the man said to him "right in the middle of the street. He was speaking with another man and turned to walk away when he was consumed by the sands and then whisked away and blown over the sea! It was the morning all of Arsinoe was found murdered and dumped into their city well"

"I am a old resident of this city. I was born and raised here with Axius as my friend!" Maurice said to the man in retort to his statements. "I am sorry that God took custody of him before I did!" Maurice added, "you mean the "Gods" don't you?" the man asked.

"I meant what I said" Maurice assured the man as he walked out of the livery and back into the streets. He resumed his walk back toward the shop of the Dolphin, except when he arrived to the shop he walked passed it and headed toward the café near the docks that he used to visit while a young man here in Pelusium.

He reached it within minutes from leaving the livery stable and could see that there were a few tables sitting out near the street and people were eating at them.

This was strange he had never seen this before. As he walked closer to the Café he saw that Adsideo was sitting at one of the three tables that was beyond the tables he had see while walking up.

It was about time that he found one of the Templars he thought to himself. He was going to ask where they had been and why they left him in that strange house without telling him where they were going. He also was wondering how they ended up in Pelusium so quickly. Maybe God's holy room was near by! Maybe through the underground hallway?

He walked up to the table from behind Adsideo and shook his chair.

"Whoa, there Maurice! It is about time. I have eaten all of the sweetbread that I can eat for a day. I have been waiting here for quite a while. I asked some of the locals where I would find someone like you and they told me that all of the locals would make it by this café at least once a day" Adsideo said to Maurice with a smile.

"Wait on me? You did not wait on me this morning!" Maurice said loud enough to make the people at the next table to take notice of them.

"I do not think you realize what has happened to us," Adsideo told him "please have a seat and have something to eat. We need to talk"

"What has happened to us?" Maurice asked, "Where are the others?"

"Our time has come, Maurice. We are to begin the task that God sat before us and each of us shall start in our birthplace. You and I are the last to begin our duties"

Adsideo began to explain "you shall try to influence the Pharaoh to accept God into his land"

"This has been tried by the mighty Moses once before and even with the miracles provided to him at that time, the Pharaoh of Egypt would not listen. Why should he listen to me?" Maurice asked Adsideo as his eyes were fixed on the food that sat on the table. Maurice raised his head and looked at Adsideo "I am not meant to be a priest Adsideo. I am a hunter and a scout. I surely cannot work the miracles of Moses either"

"You will be fine in your duties" Adsideo assured him "you are to be known as the royal hunter to Pharaoh Osorkon of the new Kingdom of Egypt. He succeeded Shishok. You are to first return the tools of the Tabernacle to Jerusalem and then try and convince Osorkon to obey by the order of men. Make him understand that he should always keep the good of the people in mind instead of greed. Teach love and patience to all that you can convince"

"I am not an ambassador nor am I a priest. I am a hunter and scout. Why can you not understand this?" Maurice said to him as he picked up the cup in front of him and filled it from the pitcher on the table.

"You will find a way to make it right for all of your kind" Adsideo told him.

"How are you so sure? I wish I was assured as you seem to be." Maurice answered back quickly.

"It will be fine. You are strong in heart as well as in will," Adsideo told him "this is a flourishing Kingdom with many ethnic groups to nourish along. You are a man of the people and you will win them over. I am sure of it and so should you"

"We were chosen by God right?" Maurice asked with a worried look on his face suddenly.

"Of course" Adsideo assured him "the eight of us with nothing better to do than keep mankind from killing it's self"

The two of them continued to chat about the adventures they had in the recent passed. They ate and drank the house wine and soon Adsideo was leaving to Tyre. He reminded Maurice of the annual meeting of the "Event" as he had explained to the others. He continued to speak of the duties morally and religiously that was to be done by the eight. He told Maurice how to get in touch with him or the other two with the powers like him.

They ended their conversation with the usual goodbyes but Maurice now seemed more assured of his task and that it would be done as foreseen by Adsideo. Maurice was told of how the estate that he woke up in had been his brother-in-laws home. The wealth to obtain it was earned by his sister and the pottery business that his mother had started. The estate was now his after the death of his brother-in-law by his own hands. This was after learning of his wife's death at Arsinoe.

"In the halls below the estate grounds you will find a Kings keep of gold and precious gems. This you will use to pay for what ever you need. I suggest that you keep it as long as possible to pay your way through life. It will be a long one" Adsideo said as he walked away from Maurice and the table at the café. Maurice sat there watching his friend leave. He waved a final goodbye but sat there thinking of their past and wondering about the future.

Maurice was to remain as an influence in North Africa throughout history. He would be known by many names famous and infamous.

Chapter Twenty-One

(Adsideo story)

Hiram, King of Tyre sat at his throne and looked over the vast model of the new palace that was to be built in his name displayed in front of him. There was to be two inlets filled in to reclaim the land from the sea. No longer would Tyre be "Two" cities divided by water it would become only one. There had always been the small island city of Tyre but as the palace expanded over time the population was pushed ashore and the merchants and ports were constructed there. But now this great plan would change this. Now Hiram would be able to closely monitor all trade traffic so that the taxes could be charged correctly. The question on his lips would be, could this be done and how much labor would this take to achieve before his death?

"Who is the master builder for this project?" Hiram asked his closest advisor.

"Why his name escapes me at this time master" the advisor replied.

"Well find out who he is now! I want to speak with him right away" Hiram said to him as he swung his scepter towards the advisor. The man went forward down the steppes leading to the throne platform and sent one of the guards to find the architect.

"Bring him here as soon as you find him" the King's advisor told the guard. Then he returned to the King's side to tell him that the architect would be brought as soon as possible.

The guard gathered three other guards and they mounted their horses and rode through the streets until they reached the Scholars school building. There they demanded that the schoolmaster to tell them of the where about of this Architect.

"The one you speak of is Zaaru-Heyan. He lives here on the campus and teaches architecture. He is a very skilled craftsman. He learned his art at Jerusalem while in charge of the construction of the holy temple there," the schoolmaster told them.

"Go and get him and tell him that King Hiram wants to see him now!" the head guard told the schoolmaster as he left them to send for the architect Zaaru-Heyan.

Soon he returned with the architect who was astounded to be taken away from his students. He was asked to look passed his anger and to ride with them to the King's palace at once.

Zaaru-Heyan met with the King that day as asked. He helped the King with the construction needs until his death. This Architect advised the King, and the Kings after him, the principals of construction as well as helping devise any subjects including the Phoenician navy, the advances in military equipment, the development of the city buildings, streets, and government put in place by one King after another and many other developments in a long line of subjects.

He changed his name many times over through out time and on the anniversary of the "event" each year he met with his fellow Templars.

As time passed the others called him many, many times. He was always there and could always come up with a reason he was away so much.

He watched his fellow Templars though out time as they too developed governments in there birthplaces. At the annual meetings they would discuss the old times but more in depth the advances in mankind as they tried in vain to keep them worthy of God.

Tyre grew to be the major port for the entire civilized world for many centuries.

From Zaaru-Heyan' s room he could view of the Mediterranean Sea. He would stand and look out of this window each night before he would go to bed. This went on for centuries but he never tired from its view. At times while in his new county he still thought of this view so much that he often finds himself standing along the coast of the sea looking from where his palace had once stood but had long since vanished.

Adsideo, Great architect of Tyre known as Zaaru-Heyan and many other famous names to come.

Chapter Twenty-Two

Democritus sat at his desk in the room above Chestnut Street and was writing in his journal. This was a trying time for all of the Templars. Not only was their work of the ages coming to a climax but there was also the new information from England that Dominic was working against the rest of the Templars.

Philadelphia
May 10th

I write this after my meeting with my fellow men of the colonies today. There was quite a bit of differences between each of the colonies representatives but for the most part I think that they are listening to us.

Afterwards Maurice met the rest of us at Carpenters hall, the other Templars and I, that is. He is not allowed to attend the meetings due to the ethnic group of his race of people. I hope to see changes in this practice of slavery and the cast of men of color as put into due to their ethnicity. These people have never heard of or seen the mighty ebony skinned Kings and Rulers I have seen through out history. Many of these would scare the life out of most of the fellow attendees of the continental congress but never the less maybe a change in this will come soon. I know that Maurice is tired of posing as my manservant but he acts content in his duties.

We have all been seeing a lot of each other lately and will continue this in the near future as they help me draft a new set of by-laws for the foundation of this country. We are using some of the better of my ideas from the Athenian and Roman republics and our own Templar laws.

I have also been writing a letter to the King, which they have been a great help with as well.

Sylvester, Laurence, and Colin were a little later arriving than the others but we began the two thousand-seven hundredth and first annual meeting of the "event". I really believe that since our loss of the old cities and the governments that this is the one that together with all of mankind behind us will truly complete our endeavors. We spoke to each other without many intrusions by the waiters and cook's help.

I hope for the sake of mankind that we are able to finally place on this earth the one government for all of the people and by the people. Time has proven to me, and I should so bravely speak for the others when I say, that despite the inability for mankind to put away their greed and ambitions to for once put their fellowman in front of these desires. Maybe with a government built of the need for these deceptive emotions of greed and ambitions shall all men feel the need to excel until they are one after the other, Kings of their own homes and may they raise as many children as there monetary means allow them to. The ones who wish not to participate shall suffer the life of a pauper while the hard working and clever shall be seen as rightful and outstanding citizens who while providing for their families will continue to provide for there nation.

Democritus signed his journal "Thomas Jefferson", his current name and closed the book for the night. He placed the book on the shelf with the other journals. Each of these with his name for that era. Many of these he had to rewrite from the many clay tablets, papaya, or scrolls which he had originally written them on.

Each of the journals was bound in the finest leathers and the covers were blank with only the name, in gold ink, on the spine to tell one from the other. He had become many different names beginning with Democritus and then on to many others after that. Each of these with its own journal. He also kept a journal for each of the other

Templars as well. These were his versions though. For some of the others have kept their own journals while others kept none at all. Democritus had thought about publishing these when the time is right.

He must wash up and prepare to meet with the others at the Apollo Tavern for a dinner meeting he thought to himself. He stood up and walked over to the window and looked down to the people passing by on Chestnut Street.

"If these people can govern themselves then any can," he thought as he looked down at them.

He must hurry and get ready to leave for the tavern for he knew that Colin, Sylvester, and Arminus must be getting back to the front lines as soon as the meeting in adjourned.

After the "accident" at Lexington last week Democritus knew that they were on an irreversible course with the war with the British.

Democritus completed his cleaning, straightened his suit jacket and began towards the door. He thought of the people of his past and the people in his present. He then walked out the door and greeted his countrymen of the future.

There outside was his new country he walked towards the Apollo Tavern. On the way he met up with Arminius, now going by the name of James Madison, and with him was Laurence. Laurence called himself John Adams during these times. Democritus noticed that Laurence was wearing the bracelet that he had picked up in the room of Temptation so many long years ago.

They walked and spoke together about the current political situation they were in with the throne of England. This included their renegade Templar brother Dominic, or at this time known as Fredrick Cornwallis archbishop of Canterbury and close adviser to King George.

"Imagine, Dominic once again was pretending to be a clergyman," Democritus thought to himself.

They soon reached the tavern and immediately went upstairs to meet the others for dinner. There sitting at the table sat Adsideo and Sylvester or in this generation commander in chief George Washington and the controversial Major General Baron Fredrick von Steuben. They were only missing Colin or known now as General Lachlan McIntosh and Adsideo told the rest of us that Colin was on his way from the front lines. He was at Fort Ticonderoga where they had been preparing for an engagement with the red coats.

It was not but about and hour later that Colin arrived and the meeting of the Templars began. They began the discussion by Democritus describing the newest events to the group. The main topic of this was Dominic's apparent alliance with the other side and the suspicion that he had turned against the Templars for good. Time would later tell that he would never again return to the Templars. Forever becoming a nemesis of all mankind.

Chapter Twenty-Three

Now as in the beginning of this story Adsideo sat above Geary Street and thought to himself about all that had transpired over the centuries. This was the strongest government on the face of the earth now and the most desirable of all.

The Soviets had fallen and proven once more that Dominic and his evil ways were destined to fail.

Adsideo thought that he had better complete getting dressed. The annual meeting of the "event" was this afternoon and he could not wait to see the others.

There was much discussion to be made at this meeting.

Dominic, having learned to deceive the Templars for so long now just may have made his last mistake. There was news that he was here in America. Sylvester had reported this from his home in New York City. If he was here he was to be found and dealt with.

Sometimes Adsideo wondered why God had allowed for Dominic to conduct his business with out the slightest reprimand. But as he had learned over time it was all up to the Templars to maintain the balance of mankind and maybe Dominic was just another adversary to be over come.

Adsideo sat down at the window seat and began to put on his Nike's. After tying the last one he looked out of the window down at the busy Geary Street. That was when he saw the man on the corner of Powell and Geary Street. This long gray haired old man was staring at Adsideo from the corner. As Adsideo adjusted his vision to close in on the man's face he saw that it was Dominic!

Adsideo jumped up from his seat and ran to the hotel door and into the hall. He would try to catch Dominic once and for all.

Once Adsideo reached the street he ran across to the opposite street corner only to find that Dominic was gone and nowhere to be seen!

Adsideo looked at his wristwatch and saw that it was time to leave for the meeting.

The sun was beginning to set over the Pacific ocean. The tall building cast a shadow over the street as Adsideo could be seen dressed in his long Londoner raincoat headed toward the Bay for his meeting of the "Event".

The End

Look for the inclusion and the conclusion to this story
coming soon.

*I am the most traveled of my contemporaries; I
have extended my field of enquiry wider than anyone else; I
have seen more countries and climes and I have heard more
speeches of learned men. No one else surpasses me in the
composition of lines according to demonstrations, not even
the Egyptian knotters of ropes or geometers.*

Democritus of Thrace

About the Author

James M. Keel was born and raised in Wichita Falls, Texas. He moved to the Dallas, Texas area in 1976 where he still resides.

He is of Chickasaw (American Indian) dissent.

James has always been a student of ancient history and ethnicity.

He also enjoys painting contemporary and traditional American Indian oil paintings.

Printed in the United States
1303100006B/13-33

9 781410 790859